A Boy
Called Lizard

by James J. Mellon

Music and Lyrics by
James J. Mellon & Scott DeTurk

Based on the Novel *Lizard* by
Dennis Covington

A SAMUEL FRENCH ACTING EDITION

SAMUEL
FRENCH

FOUNDED 1830

NEW YORK HOLLYWOOD LONDON TORONTO

SAMUELFRENCH.COM

ISBN 978-0-573-69883-5   Printed in U.S.A.   29518

RENTAL MATERIALS

An orchestration consisting of **Piano/Conductor, Drums & Percussion, Guitar/Banjo, Secondary keyboard, Bass,** and **Harmonica** will be loaned two months prior to the production ONLY on the receipt of the Licensing Fee quoted for all performances, the rental fee and a refundable deposit.

Please contact Samuel French for perusal of the music materials as well as a performance license application.

IMPORTANT BILLING AND CREDIT REQUIREMENTS

All producers of *A BOY CALLED LIZARD* must give credit to the Author of the Play in all programs distributed in connection with performances of the Play, and in all instances in which the title of the Play appears for the purposes of advertising, publicizing or otherwise exploiting the Play and/or a production. The name of the Author *must* appear on a separate line on which no other name appears, immediately following the title and *must* appear in size of type not less than fifty percent of the size of the title type.

A BOY CALLED LIZARD was first produced by the NoHo Arts Center Ensemble. The performance was directed by James J. Mellon, with sets by Craig Siebels, costumes by Shon LeBlanc, lighting by Luke Moyer, sound by Jonathan Zenz and Scott De Turk, properties design by Janet Fontaine, hair and make-up by Robin McWilliams, lizard prosthetic design by Scott Ramp, and musical direction by Robbie Gillman. The Production Stage Manager was Karesa McElheny. The cast was as follows:

CALLAHAN	James Barbour
LUCIUS SIMMS (LIZARD)	David Eldon
MISS COOLEY	Janet Fontaine
ANTON BROUSSARD	Jonathan Zenz
BUS DRIVER	Curtis C.
NURSE BARMORE	Melanie Ewbank
WALRUS	J.R. Mangels
RICARDO	Bryan Coffee
MIKE	Jonathan Zenz
MR. TINKER	Bob Morrisey
SALLY	Yvette Lawrence
MR. SIMONETTI (CALLAHAN)	James Barbour
HOMER	Jonathan Zenz
KNUTE	J.R. Mangels
RAIN	Courtney Wright
PREACHER JONES	Curtis C.
WANDA	Melanie Ewbank
EDDIE	Bryan Coffee
RHONDA	Janet Fontaine
BARTENDER	Bryan Coffee
ROBERT HOWELL	Bob Morrisey
RONNIE	Curtis C.
MIRANDA	Shannen Ferreira
WOMAN	Shannen Ferreira
BESS	Melanie Ewbank

CHARACTERS

CALLAHAN

LUCIUS SIMMS (LIZARD)

MISS COOLEY

ANTON BROUSSARD

BUS DRIVER

NURSE BARMORE

WALRUS

RICARDO

MIKE

MR. TINKER

SALLY

HOMER

KNUTE

RAIN

PREACHER JONES

WANDA

EDDIE

RHONDA

BARTENDER

ROBERT HOWELL

RONNIE

MIRANDA

WOMAN

BESS

SETTING

DeRitter, Louisiana (and other locations throughout the South)

TIME

1978

MUSICAL NUMBERS

Act I

The Ballad of Lizard. . . . . **CALLAHAN & COMPANY**

Who Are You. . . . . **MIKE, WALRUS & RICARDO**

Lullaby (Blue Skies) . . . . **LIZARD & MISS COOLEY**

Set My Spirit Free . . . . **LIZARD & COMPANY**

Set My Spirit Free (Reprise 1) . . . . **LIZARD**

Everybody Needs Shoes. . . . . **CALLAHAN & TINKER, BARMORE,**

MIKE, RICARDO & LIZARD

You're Goin' There Too . . . . **CALLAHAN, SALLY & LIZARD**

Set My Spirit Free (Reprise 2) . . . . **LIZARD**

The Silver Bowl. . . . . **RAIN & LIZARD**

Whatever I Did Know . . . . **RAIN & LIZARD**

Save Her. . . . . **CALLAHAN & LIZARD**

The Silver Bowl (Reprise) . . . . **LIZARD & RAIN**

Act II

Entr' Acte – The Ballad of Lizard (Reprise). . . . . **ORCHESTRA**

Just Imagine. . . . . **WANDA & COMPANY**

Missing Myself. . . . . **SALLY**

Everybody Needs Shoes (Reprise) . . . . **CALLAHAN**

A Tempest In The Air . . . . **COMPANY**

And So It Is . . . . **HOWELL**

Full Circle. . . . . **CALLAHAN, LIZARD & COMPANY**

To Kevin, Will & Nora, whose love brings me Full Circle every day.
With love always,
James

In loving appreciation for Kristine, who always brings me back to center.
Love,
Scott

ACT I

SCENE 1

(Prologue:)

*(Music in: a harmonica plays a musical refrain, **THE BALLAD OF LIZARD**)*

(Lights up: a pool of light illuminates a man leaning against the high branches of a giant tree.)

*(**CALLAHAN**: an actor, early to mid-40s, handsome, well built, quick to anger and passionate.)*

(Set: a tree occupies the space of the theatre creating levels, branches, areas to be converted into wherever we need to go.)

*(A young man sits on a tree stump, staring at a cigar box filled with holes. He is frozen. There is something about his look that is "off." His eyes seem too far apart, his nose squashed, his hair long and straggly. This is **LUCIUS SIMMS (LIZARD)**, an engagingly odd boy, clearly focused and awestruck at life. An air of "hope" clearly central to his demeanor. He is roughly 15.)*

(He opens the box, reaches in and pulls out a lizard (imagined). He sets it free to scamper about, always staying close, copying and mimicking it as it moves.)

CALLAHAN.

(THE BALLAD OF LIZARD)

FAT OL' LIZARD, SITTIN' ON A STUMP
GITTIN' IN HIS NOON DAY SUN
SWARM O' FLIES BUZZIN' ROUND HIS RUMP
HE'S GOT HIS EYES ON THE JUICIEST ONE
THAT OL' LIZARD...DON'T MAKE A MOVE OR HE'LL RUN

(**LUCIUS** *freezes as though the skink has stopped and is looking at him.*)

(*The surrounding area comes alive with characters.*)

CALLAHAN. *(cont'd) (addressing the audience)* I first met Lucius Simms in the summer of 1978. He was one of the kids at the Leesville School for Retarded Boys. According to his papers, no one ever proved he was retarded, like some of the others, just the way he looked made people think it. That and the fact that he didn't talk much and he spent most of his days watchin' his blue-tailed skink eat wasp larvae.
Oh yeah, a skink is a lizard.

(**LUCIUS** *scurries across the stage, eventually scurrying up the front of the tree, landing on a lower branch. He hangs down to watch the lizard pull up on his haunches. He mimics the motion.*)

ENSEMBLE.

FAT OL' LIZARD POSIN' MIGHTY STILL
FROZEN LIKE A DOG ON A QUAIL
HOLDIN' FAST, WAITIN' ON A KILL
HE'LL EAT AT LAST IF HE DON'T TWITCH HIS TAIL
THAT OL' LIZARD...DON'T EVEN BLINK OR HE'LL BAIL

(*He grabs the lizard by the tail, holding it up to look at. He begins to pet it.*)

CALLAHAN. Lucius was born in the summer of 1963 in a little town called DeRitter, Louisiana. It was one of those poor areas you'd find on the dirt roads along the Bayou. Houses with broken down porches, screen doors kicked in, flatboats overturned in the yard. Lucius lived in a one room apartment on top of the L&N Cafe. He was raised by a woman he called Miss Cooley.

(**MISS COOLEY** *enters, a slight woman, tight lipped, quick movements, wrung out hands. She is carrying a traveling bag. Behind her is* **ALTON BROUSSARD**, *a lumbering presence, keeping his distance from both* **MISS COOLEY** *and the boy.*)

MISS COOLEY. Lucius, come on down outta there. We gotta go, boy.

CALLAHAN. This whole thing began when Miss Cooley decided to send Lucius off to that State School. She was gettin' married to a gentleman who had no place for Lucius in his idea of life.

(She helps **LUCIUS** *into his backpack and the two of them start walking to the bus stop.)*

So it made sense that she was especially jittery the morning they were waiting under the awning at the DeRidder bus stop, which was really just a corner of the Texaco station next to Smitter's Barber Shop.

ALTON BROUSSARD. Alright, let's say our goodbyes and get on our way.

MISS COOLEY. He ain't never been on a bus before, you know that don't you? We have to wait here 'til it comes. I can't just leave him on the street.

*(***ALTON** *walks away from her and stares off into the distance, waiting.)*

CALLAHAN. Lucius acted like nothin' was goin' on, but underneath it all, he knew things were never gonna be the same. Hell, they both knew it.

*(***MISS COOLEY** *pins a name tag onto* **LUCIUS**' *jacket.)*

ENSEMBLE.
FAT OL' LIZARD, BITIN' ON ITS TONGUE
FIGHTIN' FOR THE RIGHT TO BE FREE
MISSED THAT FLY, OH HIS PRIDE'S BEEN STUNG
WANTIN' TO CRY, BUT HE'S JUST LIKE ME
THAT OL' LIZARD, SKIN JUST AS TOUGH AS CAN BE

*(***LUCIUS**, *who has settled onto the curb in front of the bus stop, stares up at* **MISS COOLEY**.*)*

MISS COOLEY. Now don't start that. Don't start staring at me with them eyes. It's not my fault. Alton is set in his ways. He don't want no family. He's made that clear from the very beginning. Besides, you're almost a grown man, you're gettin' to be too big to be livin' with me. You know that, right? You understand, don't you?

(beat)

MISS COOLEY.

IT DON'T WORK NO MORE
HERE WITH JUST YOU AND ME
I'VE BECOME INVISIBLE
YOU'RE ALL ANYONE CAN SEE
SO I'VE FOUND YOU A PLACE
WHERE NO ONE WHO LOOKS WILL EVEN CARE
YOU WON'T BE SO DIFFERENT THERE
YOU'LL FIT IN JUST FINE
MAYBE MAKE A FRIEND
YOU WON'T BE STUCK INSIDE ALL DAY
WAITIN' FOR THE DAY TO END
AND YOU AND I WON'T DIE FROM TRYIN' TO MAKE ENDS
    MEET
YOU'LL BE ON YOUR OWN TWO FEET
AND WE'LL BOTH GREET THAT

(The ensemble joins in on the next verse.)

SWEET TOMORROW,
AIN'T NOTHIN' LEFT BEHIND
WE BOTH GOTTA KEEP OUR MIND ON THAT
SWEET TOMORROW
THE SUN IS GONNA RISE
WE BOTH GOTTA KEEP OUR EYES ON THAT
SWEET SWEET TOMORROW

(The bus pulls up and the driver steps out. This is not meant to be realistic, a bench and a chair might be all that is required to represent the bus and the driver)

Alright now. Just do what they tell you and you'll get along fine. I'll be sure to come and visit and send you letters. We just have to give Alton time, that's all.

(helping him with his things)

There.

BUS DRIVER. I ain't got all day, lady.

MISS COOLEY. It's the Leesville State School for Retarded Boys.

BUS DRIVER. Don't you worry none. Stopped there many a time.

*(**MISS COOLEY** directs **LUCIUS** onto the bus.)*

*(**LUCIUS** starts to walk away.)*

MISS COOLEY. Hold on.

*(taking **LUCIUS** aside)*

This was the only way, Lucius. I want you to know that this was the only way I could think of for both of us.

(beat)

I know we're not prone to affection around here, but I would like, on this one occasion, if you don't mind, a hug or something. Would that be okay? Can I hug you?

*(**LUCIUS** walks back to her, still holding the box containing the lizard.)*

*(She hugs him, and **LUCIUS** begins to cry. She attempts to move him to the bus but he won't let go.)*

ALTON BROUSSARD. Hurry it up, the man's waitin' on you.

MISS COOLEY. Just give us a minute. Just one minute.

*(**MISS COOLEY** starts to cradle **LUCIUS** and sing.)*

BLUE SKIES, GREEN TREES
THERE'S A PLACE, I SEES IT IN MY MIND
NO LIES, YES PLEASE
I CAN GO THERE, FIRST I HAVE TO FIND THERE

*(**MISS COOLEY** starts to weep. **LUCIUS** gets up all on his own and walks toward the bus.)*

CALLAHAN. Lucius didn't know exactly where he was goin', n' he didn't understand quite why, but he remembered seein' in a magazine how the Mississippi was over a thousand miles long. There were supposed to be lizards in Arizona and the water up North was frozen. Perhaps he'd get to see it all through the window of this here bus.

MISS COOLEY. Alright now. Go on! And don't you go lookin' back here at any of this. We're gonna just keep our eyes forward and we'll both do fine. There's nothin' back behind. Nothin'! You remember that. Now, go on! I'll be seein' you soon.

*(**LUCIUS** joins the other passengers on the bus. They stare, some giggling. He winds up sitting alone. The bus takes off as **MISS COOLEY** fades into the darkness.)*

ENSEMBLE.

SWEET TOMORROW, IT'S JUST AROUND THE BEND
ALL OUR TROUBLES GONNA END
IN THAT SWEET TOMORROW
THERE'S NOTHIN' LEFT BEHIND
CAN'T KNOW WHAT YOU MIGHT FIND
IN THAT SWEET, SWEET TOMORROW

*(**LUCIUS** arrives at the Leesville State School. The students surround him. They include: **WALRUS** [an introvert - always listening to his radio, music his security blanket], **MIKE** [**WALRUS**' brother, high energy, short attention, extremely insecure - his one job to look after his brother], **RICARDO** [a loud-mouthed bully, short fuse and proud of it - but deep down a caring heart - mostly misunderstood, he acts out the misunderstanding with rage.])*

*(The **BOYS** are all staring at **LUCIUS** as though they haven't ever seen anyone so "strange" before.)*

*(**NURSE BARMORE** enters in a sweeping motion, breaking up the crowd. She is a "sturdy" woman, with a "take charge" personality.)*

NURSE. Alright, alright, nothin' to look at. Quit your starin'. Ain't polite.

*(The **KIDS** stare at him and laugh, building into...)*

WALRUS. What the hell is it? Look at his eyes!

NURSE. None of that, Walrus. Get back there with the others. I mean it. This instant!

*(**LUCIUS** is staring at **RICARDO**, concerned.)*

RICARDO. What you lookin' at, freak? We're the ones should be doin' the lookin'!

NURSE. Ricardo! Would you like a trip to the "quiet room."

RICARDO. Only if you come in there with me.

MIKE. *(playing out a scene)* Ooooh...Nurse Barmaid...give me big ol' smooch right on my lips.

*(The boys laugh. **NURSE** looks at each of them, shutting them up one by one with only a look.)*

*(***WALRUS** puts his radio up to his ear and escapes into his music.)*

*(***NURSE** takes **LUCIUS** by the hand and walks him over to the sleeping quarters.)*

NURSE. *(to **LUCIUS***)* Watch your step. Don't want you breakin' anything 'til we know you better. This here's your room, shared with the other boys. This your locker. All belongin's go in here. Empty it all out and come on downstairs meet the others.

(beat)

You're gonna like it here. You'll see. We're just one big ol' family.

*(The **NURSE** leaves **LUCIUS** alone and exits.)*

ENSEMBLE.

FAT OL' LIZARD, SCAMPERED CROSS THE ROAD
HAMPERED BY THE MID-DAY GLARE
LEFT BEHIND MOST EVERTHING HE KNOW'D
WHAT WILL HE FIND IF HE MAKES IT OVER THERE
THAT OL' LIZARD, AIN'T NO ONE LEFT WHO MIGHT CARE

*(***LUCIUS** returns to the schoolyard. The kids start to circle him, laughing and keeping their distance as if he were an alien. **LUCIUS** carries his box with him.)*

FAT OL' LIZARD, THROWN INTO A BOX
WITH ROCKS AND TWIGS AND FOUR CARDBOARD WALLS
DOESN'T KNOW EXACTLY WHERE TO RUN
HE'D LIKE TO GO BUT HE CAN'T FIND THE SUN

ENSEMBLE.

> THAT OL' LIZARD, AIN'T LIKELY HE'LL HAVE MUCH FUN
> HE'S DONE BEFORE HE'S BEGUN
> IF HE LOSE FAITH IN THAT SWEET, SWEET TOMORROW
>
> *(A whistle is blown and the boys all run into place at the dinner table.)*

SCENE 2

(The boys make it very clear that **LUCIUS** *is not welcome to sit with their group.)*

(A man enters and speaks to the kids. He is **MR. TINKER**, *odd character with visibly smelly clothing, wire glasses and a nervousness not easily controlled.)*

MR. TINKER. Alright, listen up.

(No one pays him much mind. He eventually hits a table with a large stick.)

Silence!

There's not gonna be any bingo tonight.

(they all moan)

No one to call the numbers. Miss Rose had her an "incident" and she's off takin' care of it.

MIKE. That's bullshit.

WALRUS. What's an "incident?"

RICARDO. Mean's she's crazier than us.

MR. TINKER. We'll be goin' swimmin' down at the hole tomorrow mornin' so come to breakfast with your swim trunks on under your clothes. If you forget 'em, you can sit on the dirt n' just watch. And NO you cannot swim naked. Anyone caught swimmin' without trunks will spend the rest of the week in the "quiet room." Clear?

RICARDO. *(referring to* **LUCIUS***)* What about him? We gotta swim with him?

MR. TINKER. Mr. Simms, why don't you say something about yourself.

*(***LUCIUS** *just stares at them all. Words don't come out. The boys start to laugh.)*

WALRUS. Turdhead can't talk.

MR. TINKER. I'm sure Mr. Simms can talk when he wants to. Isn't that right Mr. Simms?

WALRUS. Isn't that right, Mr. Simms?

> *(Quiet.* **LUCIUS** *doesn't talk, the boys just laugh.)*

MR. TINKER. Alright, everyone out in the yard. Anyone caught fightin' loses smokin' privileges for a week.

> *(The action shifts to the yard.)*

> *(MUSIC IN: **WHO ARE YOU**)*

> *(***LUCIUS** *follows the other outside to the yard. He walks away from them and tries to sit by himself. They creep closer until they are practically on top of him.)*

RICARDO.

> *(**WHO ARE YOU**)*

> MAMMA LEFT ME ON THE STEPS OF THE FIRST BAPTIST
>   CHURCH
> WHEN I WAS ONLY SIX MONTHS OLD
> THAT BITCH DITCHED ME ON CHRISTMAS
> DIDN'T EVEN LEAVE A GIFT
> JUST A PIECE OF SHIT BLANKET
> BETWEEN ME AND THE COLD

MIKE.

> OUR OLD MAN HE UP AND SPLIT, LEFT MY BROTHER AND ME
> IN THE BATHROOM OF SOME PISSHOLE BAR
> DIDN'T LEAVE US NO MONEY
> DON'T KNOW WHERE THAT MOTHA' WENT
> HOPE HE'S DEAD IN SOME HELLHOLE
> BECAUSE THAT'S WHERE WE ARE

WALRUS.

> WHO ARE YOU, YOU A RETARD
> ARE YOU CRAZY - OR JUST FAKIN'
> YOU A FREAK, OR JUST UGLY
> ONE THING SURE YOU'RE MAKIN' ME SICK

ALL THREE.

> WHO ARE YOU, YOU'RE AN ASSHOLE
> WHERE'S YOUR TONGUE, DO YOU GOT ONE
> DID YOU BITE IT, DID YOU SWALLOW
> TELL US WHAT WE'RE NEEDIN'
> DON'T BE FEEDIN' US NO SHIT, YOU TWIT
> WHO ARE YOU

*(**LUCIUS** tries to escape from them. They follow him.)*

MIKE. I bit the barber so bad he cried. A grown man, and he cried like a baby.

WALRUS. I bit Nurse Barmaid. She squealed like a pig.

RICARDO. I drink whisky before breakfast and anybody who says I don't, I give them this.

(He puts his fist up.)

MIKE. I've been to Galveston. I danced naked in the middle of the street.

RICARDO. I been smokin' weed since I was six.

MIKE. You ask anyone, they know who Mike is.

WALRUS. I tripped Nurse Barmaid, chipped her tooth on the floor. I'll do it again. I'm not afraid. That's who I am.

ALL THREE.

WHO ARE YOU, COME ON TELL US
WHERE'S YOUR PLANET

WALRUS.

IT'S URANUS

(They all laugh.)

ALL THREE.

YOU'RE A WEIRDO, WHAT'S YOUR SECRET
HEY, SIDE SHOW, ENTERTAIN US
WE'RE INSANE, NOT JUST SOME PAINS IN THE ASS

MIKE.

YOU GOT A SISTER
IS HER FACE ALL BLISTER PUSS LIKE YOURS

WALRUS.

DID SOMEONE SMASH YOU IN THE FACE

RICARDO.

THAT SPACE BETWEEN YOUR EYES IS SCARY

MIKE.

LOOK, YOU HAIRY LITTLE TURD

RICARDO.

COME ON YOU FREAK, JUST SPEAK A WORD

ALL THREE.
> BEFORE WE SPILL YOUR PUNY BRAIN
> AND STAIN THE MUD WITH YOUR BLOOD
> YOU CRUD, YOU ALIEN, SCALIAN, REPTAILIAN LOOKIN'...

WALRUS. *(spoken)* Lizard!

MIKE. Oh shit, he does look like a lizard.

RICARDO. He does. Look at his eyes.

MIKE. That's your new name, Lizard.

> *(The boys run around him trying to get him to focus on them with his crossed eyes. They continue to laugh and dance around as the music builds to a climax.)*

ALL THREE.
> WHO ARE YOU

RICARDO. Come on, say somethin'!

MIKE. You don't talk? Is that it?

RICARDO. The buck-teethed Albinos'll make you talk. You'll see.

MIKE. They can disappear through walls. They're freaks.

RICARDO. I'm not afraid of 'em though.

MIKE. Ricardo's not afraid of anything.

> *(**WALRUS** puts his radio to his head and starts to zone out. **RICARDO** watches for the others.)*

RICARDO. 'Cept for the creep with no hands. He ain't afraid of nothin'. You'd think if you didn't have any hands you might think twice before gettin' into a fight. Jerk bit me on the back and I couldn't get at him cause he held onto my skin. Bit clear through to the bone. Then he held onto that.

MIKE. We call him "Dog" since he wouldn't let go of 'Cardo's bone.

RICARDO. They had to shoot him with a needle to get him off.

> *(**WALRUS**' music has stopped and he starts to whine... slow at first and then with more and more panic. **MIKE** runs over and tries to fix the radio. It's dead. **RICARDO** tries to touch **WALRUS** but he pushes him across the floor.)*

(**WALRUS** *starts to pound on the walls and begins a tirade of throwing anything in his way.* **MR. TINKER** *enters and grabs hold of* **WALRUS**.)

MR. TINKER. Stop him!

(**NURSE BARMORE** *enters and immediately tries to grab* **WALRUS**. *He throws her to the ground and pounces on her.*)

(**MR. TINKER** *tries to pull them apart. He and* **NURSE BARMORE** *have* **WALRUS** *in a lock hold for the moment.* **MIKE** *jumps in.*)

MIKE. Leave him alone. Walrus! Stop! Stop before they hurt you.

MR. TINKER. *(to* **MIKE**) Where's his radio?

MIKE. He threw it over there.

MR. TINKER. Go get it.

RICARDO. I think it might need new batteries.

MR. TINKER. Mike, there's some batteries in the top drawer of my desk. Get 'em. Now!

(*As* **TINKER** *and* **BARMORE** *attempt to hold* **WALRUS** *down,* **LUCIUS** *walks forward and starts to sing.*)

LUCIUS.

(LULLABYE)

BLUE SKIES, GREEN TREES
THERE'S A PLACE, I SEES IT IN MY MIND
NO LIES, YES PLEASE
I CAN GO THERE, FIRST I HAVE TO FIND THERE
IN THE BLUE SKIES, GREEN SEAS
TAKE ME BACK, JUST SAIL ACROSS THE MOON
AND SOON ALL THAT WILL BE LEFT
IS NOTHING BUT THOSE BLUE SKIES

(*Everyone has stopped to listen to* **LUCIUS** *sing. His voice is sweet and pure and completely authentic.* **WALRUS** *stops fighting and calmly sits on the ground beside* **LUCIUS**.)

NURSE. Sing it again, Lucius.

> (**LUCIUS** *sings the song again, as he does,* **MISS COOLEY** *appears in a pool of light. She sings with him.*)

LUCIUS & MISS COOLEY.

> BLUE SKIES, GREEN TREES
> THERE'S A PLACE, I SEES IT IN MY MIND
> NO LIES, YES PLEASE
>
> I CAN GO THERE, FIRST I HAVE TO FIND THERE
> IN THE BLUE SKIES, GREEN SEAS
> TAKE ME BACK, JUST SAIL ACROSS THE MOON
> AND SOON ALL THAT WILL BE LEFT
> IS NOTHING BUT THOSE BLUE SKIES

> (**MIKE** *enters with batteries.* **RICARDO** *brings him the radio and they put it back together. They are all amazed at* **LUCIUS***'s voice. They hand the radio back to* **WALRUS** *and he holds it tight against his head.*)

NURSE. Good job, Lucius. You got an angel gift with that voice.

(to the others)

Alright, everyone. Show's over. Go about your business. Nothing to see here. Get along to your business.

MR. TINKER. *(to* **LUCIUS***)* Thanks, Lucius.

> (**MIKE** *comes over and puts his arm around* **LUCIUS**.)

MIKE. He likes to be called Lizard.

MR. TINKER. That so? Well, you boys watch out for him.

> (**MR. TINKER** *and* **NURSE BARMORE** *exit.*)

> (**RICARDO** *and* **MIKE** *cross to* **WALRUS** *to make sure he's okay. MUSIC:* ***LULLABYE.*** *The boys exit.*)

> (**LUCIUS** *trails behind, looks around and climbs the tree with his box.*)

> *(Lights fade to night.)*

> *(Off in the distance we can hear people calling:)*

NURSE. *(offstage)* Lucius Simms! Lucius, come on out boy!

MIKE. *(offstage)* Lizard! Where you hidin'?

WALRUS. *(offstage)* Lizard! Come on, we're tired.

(**MR. TINKER** *comes out and sees* **LUCIUS** *in the tree.*)

MR. TINKER. You gonna stay up there all night? It's gonna get cold.

(no answer)

Suit yourself. We're all goin' to bed. Doors'll be locked. You'll sleep out here.

(The lights fade on **LUCIUS** *as he falls asleep in the tree.)*

SCENE 3

(Next Morning:)

*(**MIKE, RICARDO** and **WALRUS** come running onstage.
They see **LUCIUS** up in the tree and start talking to him
[this is a regular thing].)*

MIKE. Lizard, you been up there all night?

*(**LUCIUS** nods.)*

MIKE. *(cont'd)* Well come on down, I gotta tell you about
the lady in the parking lot. She was wearin' this slinky
robe and she had the most beautiful "wheels" I ever
seen.

RICARDO. They're the only "wheels" you ever seen.

MIKE. You know that's not true. I had sex already, you know
that.

WALRUS. Dreamin' sex don't count.

MIKE. What do you know about it anyway, just listen to your
radio.

RICARDO. There's two of 'em in a trailer. Actors! I heard
'em rehearsin'. They're gonna do a show for us today
in the gym.

*(MUSIC IN: **THE BALLAD OF LIZARD**)*

*(**LUCIUS** climbs down from the tree and helps the boys set
up the chairs for the show. **MR. TINKER** enters dressed in
pirates clothing. The boys laugh and make fun. It takes
a moment but he finally gets them quieted (sort of). He
addresses the school.)*

MR. TINKER. Alright, settle down. After the show you each
can have one candy bar or a pack of gum. One or the
other, not both. And there's no Snickers tonight so
don't ask for 'em.

(moaning from the crowd)

And those over fourteen are eligible for cigarettes,
ELIGIBLE, doesn't mean you get'em, just means

you're ELIGIBLE. Depends on how well behaved you are during the play. Anything flies across this room, and I don't care how "small" it is, your privileges are history.

(beat)

(The lights go to black.)

*(MUSIC IN: **TREASURE ISLAND MUSIC**)*

*(A boy (**SALLY AS JIM HAWKINS**) and an old man (**CALLAHAN AS LONG JOHN SILVER**) appear in a pool of light. The boy is young and innocent looking, but with a twinkle in his eye and a "Peter Pan" quality in his walk. The old man supports long grey hair, a beard, and a prominent scar across his cheek.)*

JIM HAWKINS (SALLY). I am your servant, Jim Hawkins. And I have seen a world of woes.

(referring to the old man)

This is where it all began, with a pirate by the name of...

*(**CALLAHAN** throws off the old man costume and under it is dressed in pirate regalia.)*

LONG JOHN SILVER (CALLAHAN). LONG JOHN SILVER!

*(The boys shriek in fun and fright. **JIM HAWKINS** jumps to another platform.)*

*(**LONG JOHN SILVER** pulls a knife and holds **JIM HAWKINS** prisoner.)*

LONG JOHN SILVER. *(cont'd)* I'll give you one more chance to tell me where the treasure is hidden.

JIM HAWKINS. Don't hurt me! I'll tell you everything. The treasure is buried on a place called Treasure Island.

LONG JOHN SILVER. Where exactly is this Treasure Island, you filthy boy?

JIM HAWKINS. It's at the farthest edge of the ocean.

LONG JOHN SILVER. Ho-ho! That's all I wanted to know, mate!

(**LONG JOHN SILVER** *pulls a gun out of his coat and points it at* **JIM HAWKINS**)

(The boys in the gym cry out for him: "Watch out!" "Don't do it!")

JIM HAWKINS. Sir, if you take me with you, I can guide you to it.

LONG JOHN SILVER. Why do I need you?

JIM HAWKINS. The farthest edge of the ocean's a big place. I can lead you to the exact marking.

(**LONG JOHN SILVER** *now has the gun right up to his temple.*)

LONG JOHN SILVER. The fun's in the search, boy. No such thing as exact!

(He cranks the gun. The boys go wild as the lights go to silhouette and the action begins to play out in slow motion.)

(A light comes up on **LUCIUS**, *entranced by the show...he sings* ***SET MY SPIRIT FREE***)

LUCIUS.

(*SET MY SPIRIT FREE*)

I NEVER SAW ANYTHING LIKE THAT BEFORE
HOW IT SET MY MIND TO RACING
IT DROPPED MY JAW, I SWEAR IT WAS ON THE FLOOR
SUDDENLY I SEE A DREAM WORTH CHASING

EVERY FACE THEY'D MAKE, EVERY DOUBLE TAKE
EVERY NOTE THEY SANG HAD ME SQUEALING
EVERY WORD I HEARD SEEMED FOR MY OWN SAKE
EVERYTHING THEY FELT, I WAS FEELING

WANNA GO WHERE THEY GO, SEE WHAT THEY SEE
KNOW WHAT THEY KNOW, WHERE LIFE TAKES ME
LET IT SHOW ME WHAT IT MEANS TO BE
IN A WORLD WHERE I CAN SET MY SPIRIT FREE

(The story begins to play out beyond the storytelling. The entire stage turns into Treasure Island, *all the boys taking part in the adventure. [NOTE: this can be done*

with the imagination, or with special effects. It is most important that what we see onstage visually matches what **LUCIUS** *is experiencing in his mind.])*

THE WORLD I'VE MADE'S ALWAYS BEEN WITHIN FOUR
    WALLS
NEVER TRIED TO SEE WHAT'S OUT THERE
BEEN TOO AFRAID OF THE STUMBLES AND THE FALLS
GOTTA SUDDEN URGE FOR GOIN' SOMEWHERE

WHERE THE EAGLE FLIES OVER PRAIRIE SKIES
AND THE RIVERS RUN ON FOREVER
WHERE THE GRAY GIVES WAY TO A PINK SUNRISE
THE HORIZON SEEMS IT WILL NEVER END

HAVE TO FIND IT, TIME'S A WASTIN'
I'M BEHIND, IT'S TIME FOR TASTIN'
EVERYTHING THAT'S WAITIN' THERE FOR ME
IN A WORLD WHERE I CAN SET MY SPIRIT FREE

*(***LUCIUS*** becomes involved with the story itself, singing as he interacts with the others.)*

LUCIUS.

MY IMAGINATION'S ON FIRE
MY HEAD IS FULL OF PICTURES
AND MY HEART'S FULL OF DESIRE
AND I KNOW I WON'T SLEEP TONIGHT
CAUSE THE DREAM I'M DREAMIN' CAN'T COME TRUE
'TIL I SEE IT IN THE MORNING'S LIGHT

I'VE NEVER FELT ANYTHING LIKE THIS BEFORE
IT'S LIKE THERE'S SOMEONE ELSE INSIDE ME
HE'S CAST A SPELL, TUGGIN' ME RIGHT THROUGH THE
    DOOR
ALL I NEED'S SOMEBODY'S HAND TO GUIDE ME

TO EXOTIC LANDS SEARCHING ISLAND STRANDS
FIND WHERE PIRATES BURIED THEIR TREASURE
WAND'RING FANCY FREE ACROSS DESERT SANDS
NO DEMANDS EXCEPT FINDIN' PLEASURE

WANNA SEE IT, HEAR IT, MAKE IT REAL
IT SEEMS SO NEAR IT'S LIKE I FEEL IT
TAKIN' OVER EVERY PART OF ME

IN A WORLD, WHERE THERE AIN'T NOTHIN' I CAN'T BE
THERE'S A WORLD, WHERE I CAN SET MY SPIRIT FREE

*(By the conclusion of the song, we are right back where
we started. The* **ACTORS** *are taking their bows and the
boys are disbanding.)*

*(***LUCIUS*** begins to sword fight and interact with the
kids.* **MR. TINKER** *comes out and calls them inside [we
don't need to hear this].)*

*(***LUCIUS*** hangs back, like before, and climbs his tree.)*

SCENE 4

(From the position in the tree he can now see into the trailer of the actors. He climbs to a better branch for hearing.)

CALLAHAN. I have to admit it, Sally. You were right. I thought it was stupid, us comin' here, but those kids were the best audience we've ever had.

SALLY. I don't know if that says more about them or us.

CALLAHAN. You think they understood it?

SALLY. Don't underestimate them. They understand more than we do.

CALLAHAN. What was that smell?

SALLY. I think they call it, Institute.

CALLAHAN. Aren't they supposed to take care of them? I mean, the whole place feels like a prison.

SALLY. Well, they all seemed to be having a good time.

(SALLY, who has been disrobing throughout, pulls off her blouse, leaving her in bra and pants.)

(The audience now recognizes that the boy playing JIM HAWKINS is actually, SALLY, early 30s, beautiful, strong, down to earth sensibility.)

(The old man playing LONG JOHN SILVER is actually CALLAHAN. We can see that he and SALLY are a couple.)

(LUCIUS is embarrassed by what he sees, and yet he cannot turn away. He is in awe of her beauty and in touch with his own feelings.)

(He lets out an involuntary sigh.)

LUCIUS. *(under his breath)* Wow!

(Beat. SALLY listens.)

SALLY. Cal, did you hear that?

CALLAHAN. What?

SALLY. I think someone's out there.

(**CALLAHAN** *sticks his head out from the space and comes face to face with* **LUCIUS**. *He recoils and pulls away.*)

CALLAHAN. Holy shit!

SALLY. *(frightened)* What is it?

CALLAHAN. *(to* **SALLY***)* One 'o them kids from the school. Looks like he's been beat up. *(to* **LUCIUS***)* Are you alright?

(**LUCIUS** *doesn't speak at first, trying to bring words to his mouth. He merely stutters...*)

LUCIUS. Uh...

CALLAHAN. Do you need help? Did someone do that to your face?

LUCIUS. *(softly)* No...

CALLAHAN. Okay...so...what do you want?

LUCIUS. *(beat)* I...ah...

CALLAHAN. It's okay. We're not gonna bite you.

(**LUCIUS** *jumps through the window, landing on the floor. He looks up at them and explodes with excitement.*)

LUCIUS. I...wanna go with you.

CALLAHAN. You want to go with us, where?

LUCIUS. Don't matter.

(**SALLY** *crosses to* **CALLAHAN** *and looks at* **LUCIUS**. *Her reaction is more concern than fright.*)

SALLY. What happened to you?

LUCIUS. Nothin' happened to me.

(beat)

That's why I wanna come with you. I want things to happen to me. I want to search for buried treasure like Jim Hawkins and see the world, and...

SALLY. *(as if to a child)* But that was just a story. We're actors. You understand that, don't you? We're not searching for buried treasure.

CALLAHAN. It just feels like that most o' the time.

LUCIUS. I'm not like the rest of them. In case you were worried. I'm not retarded.

SALLY. Okay.

(beat)

What's your name?

LUCIUS. Lizard!

SALLY. That's it? Just Lizard?

LUCIUS. Lizard Simms.

CALLAHAN. Okay, Lizard Simms. What can you offer us?

SALLY. Cal! That's not funny.

CALLAHAN. Well, he wants to come with us. What would we get out of it?

SALLY. Cal!

LUCIUS. I could cook, clean, carry things for you.

CALLAHAN. I have Sally here for all of that. What else?

LUCIUS. I could make props 'n costumes. I'm good with my hands. I could...

(He's at a loss.)

SALLY. *(to CAL)* Alright, that's enough. *(to LUCIUS)* I'm sorry. We can't be takin' you with us. That's just not possible.

LUCIUS. Why? I won't be any trouble. I promise. Please. If it don't work out you can just drop me off wherever you decide.

*(**SALLY** doesn't know what to say. She looks to **CAL**, who is no help. She looks back to **LUCIUS**, so hopeful.)*

CALLAHAN. Look, you'd better go on back to your room. It's gettin' late. You shouldn't be out here.

LUCIUS. *(desperate)* I CAN SING!

*(The desperation in his voice stops both **SALLY** and **CALLAHAN** for a moment. **SALLY** catches herself and continues.)*

CALLAHAN. And I'm sure you have a nice sound. But ain't you supposed to be somewhere right now? Someone's gonna be lookin' for you pretty soon. And I would rather them not find you here.

(to **SALLY***)*

That man, Tinker, told us not to talk to 'em. Remember?

SALLY. Since when do you listen to what anyone tells you to do?

LUCIUS. Please take me with you. I don't belong here.

CALLAHAN. Happens to all of us, kid, you just have to make the best of it. I'm sorry. Now go on.

*(***LUCIUS*** tries one more time to speak, but* **CALLAHAN** *stops him.)*

Go on!

*(***LUCIUS*** turns and runs off.)*

*(MUSIC: **THE BALLAD OF LIZARD**)*

CALLAHAN. *(cont'd)* Now that's a first. They don't usually want to come home with us. We must be gettin' better.

SALLY. What's a boy like that doin' here? It breaks my heart.

CALLAHAN. Where else would they put him with a face like that?

SALLY. What do you think happened to it?

CALLAHAN. Probably born that way.

SALLY. Don't feel right. Him bein' here.

CALLAHAN. Yeah, well, he'll be alright. Let's not go gettin' involved.

SALLY. You know what I was thinkin'? We have to find someone to replace Jerry in *The Tempest*, right?

CALLAHAN. Yeah...so?

SALLY. Maybe that kid could play Caliban.

CALLAHAN. *(laughing)* You're not serious.

SALLY. I am. People would pay good money to see a boy like that. He could help us and we could help him.

CALLAHAN. No! That's just a bad idea.

SALLY. I think we should take him with us.

CALLAHAN. Yeah, okay. In fact, let's take them all with us. Let's just have ourselves our very own Greek chorus.

SALLY. I'm serious.

CALLAHAN. You are not.

SALLY. I am.

CALLAHAN. You can't just take a kid out of a state institute. Besides the obvious fact that I don't know why you'd want to...they don't just hand them over to perfect strangers.

SALLY. I think you're missing an opportunity here. Think about it. What're you gonna tell Wanda when you show up without a Caliban?

(CALLAHAN looks at her with a twinkle in his eye. He's thinking about it.)

CALLAHAN. You really think that kid can play Caliban in *The Tempest?*

SALLY. Yeah, he won't even need makeup.

(A pool of light hits LUCIUS, nestled in the top branches of his tree.)

*(MUSIC IN: **SET MY SPIRIT FREE - Reprise**)*

CALLAHAN. So how do we do this?

SALLY. Oh, I'm sure you can think of something.

(The lights fade on CALLAHAN and SALLY, as they plot their next move.)

(LUCIUS, staring at the sky, sings:)

LUCIUS.
WANNA SEE IT, HEAR IT, MAKE IT REAL
IT SEEMS SO NEAR IT'S LIKE I FEEL IT
TAKING OVER EVERY PART OF ME
IN A WORLD, WHERE IT DON'T MATTER WHAT THEY SEE
THERE'S A WORLD, WHERE I CAN SET MY SPIRIT FREE

(Lights shift: A short while later.)

SCENE 5

(MIKE, WALRUS and RICARDO run onto the stage and to the bottom of the tree. They're in swim trunks and are holding towels. RICARDO has a bandage on his right knee. They look up the tree and find LUCIUS on one of the branches.)

MIKE. You talk to them actors?

LUCIUS. One of 'em was a woman.

MIKE. *(to RICARDO)* I told you. I can spot a set of wheels no matter how much they're covered up.

LUCIUS. *(to RICARDO)* What happened to you?

RICARDO. One of the midgets bit me at breakfast.

MIKE. I'm sure it tasted better 'n what they were servin'.

WALRUS. Barmaid's lookin' for you.

MIKE. You got a visitor.

LUCIUS. Who?

WALRUS. Some guy.

(NURSE BARMORE enters and walks directly over to the tree. She is clearly not happy.)

NURSE. Lucius Simms, you come down from that tree before I have a chance to take another breath.

LUCIUS. No.

(The boys laugh. NURSE BARMORE swings around on her heels.)

NURSE. The rest of you want to lose your swimin' privileges?

MIKE. Nothin' wrong with climbin' a tree.

NURSE. Where's it say that? I want you to show me where it says that.

RICARDO. It says it right up here on my lips.

NURSE. That's enough.

(to LUCIUS)

You oughtta choose a better group of boys to hang around with.

WALRUS. Yeah, maybe he could hang out with the albinos and learn how to walk through walls.

NURSE. Alright, enough of that. Your father's here to see you.

(All the boys, including **LUCIUS,** *freeze.)*

LUCIUS. Who?

NURSE. You heard me. Now climb down outta that tree and get your butt into the shower. You stink. I can smell you from here.

(She turns and begins to exit.)

LUCIUS. My daddy's dead.

NURSE. Don't tell him that.

(She exits.)

WALRUS. You really think it's him?

MIKE. Maybe he has a lot of money.

RICARDO. Won't you know him when you see him? When was the last time...

LUCIUS. *(screaming)* HE'S DEAD!

*(***MR. TINKER** *enters with a longnosed guy wearing glasses and a mustache. He's got a head of bushy blonde hair stuffed into a hat. His walk is stiff and awkward. His name is* **MR. SIMONETTI (CALLAHAN).** *)*

*(***TINKER** *leads him to the tree and points up to the branch where* **LUCIUS** *is sitting.)*

MR. SIMONETTI (CALLAHAN). Lucius? You don't know me. My name is Simonetti, Harold Simonetti.

(The boys laugh at the name Harold.)

WALRUS. Harold!

MR. SIMONETTI. Yeah, that was a hard one growing up. But I'm pretty good with it now. Harold is okay. Anyway, I'm from Brooklyn, New York. Can you hear me okay from up there?

(He doesn't respond.)

I drove all the way here from Massachusetts to see you.
I'm a shoe salesman, so I'm wastin' good sellin' time,
not that this is a waste, but I'm just a regular guy, and I
really want to talk to you so what do you say, boy, how
about comin' down and lettin' me get a good up close
look at you?

(**LUCIUS** *stares straight ahead and doesn't respond.* **MR.
SIMONETTI** *turns and looks at* **TINKER,** *who steps to
the bottom of the tree.*)

MR. TINKER. Lucius, I want you to think carefully. A woman
named Cooley signed your papers. She any relation to
you?

LUCIUS. No.

MR. TINKER. You lived with her, right?

LUCIUS. Yes.

MR. TINKER. But you're not related to her?

LUCIUS. No.

MR. TINKER. She ever mention Mr. Simonetti?

LUCIUS. No.

MR. TINKER. Did anybody?

LUCIUS. No.

MR. TINKER. What's your Dad's name then?

MIKE. Sure as hell ain't Harold.

(*The boys laugh. So does* **HAROLD.**)

RICARDO. He never knew his dad's name. He died when he
was born, ain't that right Lizard?

MR. TINKER. (*to* **LUCIUS**) Didn't you ever think to ask?

MR. SIMONETTI. Stop badgering the boy. He told you what
he knows.

MR. TINKER. I'm just trying to jog his memory. He's
retarded you know.

MR. SIMONETTI. He don't seem retarded to me.

(*Beat.* **TINKER** *looks at* **SIMONETTI** *as if he's recogniz-
ing him.*)

LUCIUS. My daddy weren't no shoe salesman.

MR. SIMONETTI. You got somethin' against shoes?

LUCIUS. No!

MR. SIMONETTI. I hope not. Everybody needs shoes. Isn't that right, Mr. Tinkle?

(The boys laugh. He's winning them over.)

MR. TINKER. Tinker. You know you look familiar to me. Have we met before?

*(MUSIC IN: **EVERYBODY NEEDS SHOES**)*

MR. SIMONETTI. Can't say we have.

MR. TINKER. I never forget a face.

MR. SIMONETTI. Funny, I never forget a foot.

*(looking down at **TINKER** 's foot)*

Have we met before? You look awfully familiar to me.

(The boys laugh at this idea as he sets up his soap box, of shoes.)

MR. SIMONETTI. *(cont'd)* How you been feeling lately?

MR. TINKER. You mean my feet?

MR. SIMONETTI. Oh no, not just your feet?

(he sings)

(EVERYBODY NEEDS SHOES)

EVERYBODY KNOWS, COMFORT STARTS IN YOUR TOES
AND GOES UP THROUGH THE SOLES OF YOUR FEET
GOTTA HAVE A GOOD FOUNDATION
AND I'LL STAKE MY REPUTATION
I'M THE BEST AT GIVIN' YOUR DOGS A TREAT
WHERE THE LEATHER GOES TO MEET THE STREET

I GOT WINGTIPS AND LOAFERS
OXFORDS AND MOCS
LACES AND POLISH
GARTERS AND SOCKS

OH I GOTS WHAT YOU'RE NEEDIN'
IF YOUR CORN STARTS TO OOZE

COME TO ME, I'M THE MAN
OH YEAH!
EVERYBODY NEEDS SHOES

*(**NURSE BARMORE** enters and **MR. SIMONETTI** takes
her in his arms, singing the next verse to her. The boys
love it.)*

I GOT BUCKLES AND BRACES
PATENS AND PEARLS
ROCKERS LOVE BLUE SUEDE
WORKS ON THE GIRLS

I GOT FLUFFIES FOR MOMMA
AND HER HOUSEWIFE BLUES
COME TO ME, I'M THE MAN
OH YEAH!
EVERY MAMMA NEEDS SHOES

OH IT MIGHT NOT SEEM EXCITIN'
I KNOW IT SEEMS ODD
BUT A FOOT IS LIKE A PIECE OF PIE
IT'S WARM AND IT'S INVITIN'
CRUSTY AND SWEET
AND ONCE YOUR FINGER'S TOUCH THOSE FEET
I SWEAR YOU'LL GET TO MEET GOD

*(**MR. SIMONETTI** dances to prove his point about feet.
Little by little, **LUCIUS** joins the others and is drawn
into **HAROLD**'s performance.)*

I GOT EIGHT HOLES AND TEN HOLES
TIES UP THE LEG
VELCROS AND SPRING SOLES, HOSE IN AN EGG
I GOT RATTLESNAKE LEATHERS
THAT YOUR TOES CAN'T REFUSE
COME TO ME, YOU CAN'T LOSE
BRING YOUR FEET IN ANY SIZE
FROM ONE A'S TO TWENTY TWO DOUBLE U'S
COME TO ME, I'M THE MAN, OH YEAH
I'LL HELP YOU COPE WITH EVERY
BUNION, BLISTER, CALLOUS AND BRUISE

COME TO ME, I'M THE MAN, OH YEAH
EVERYBODY NEEDS SHOES

(After the song, **LUCIUS** *is clearly more "open" to exploring this possible "relationship.")*

MR. TINKER. *(to* **LUCIUS***)* Harold, would you like to come with us to the lake this afternoon? Spend a little time with Lucius?

MR. SIMONETTI. It would be my pleasure. *(to* **LUCIUS***)* That okay with you?

(long beat)

LUCIUS. I don't care.

(MUSIC: ***EVERYBODY NEEDS SHOES*** */ into* ***THE BALLAD OF LIZARD****)*

(The scene shifts to the lake. The boys all run off to the water as **LUCIUS** *and* **MR. SIMONETTI** *continue their discussion.)*

SCENE 6

(**MR. TINKER** *stays a step or two behind, able to hear what's going on but also paying attention to the other boys.*)

MR. TINKER. You boys don't go too far out. Stay in the shallow end and no dunkin' each other. N' take off your trunks if you're gonna piss in the water. But put 'em back on before you get out. And I mean it.

MR. SIMONETTI. You don't like swimmin'? Figure with a name like Lizard...

LUCIUS. *(beat)* You really a shoe salesman?

MR. SIMONETTI. Sure am, but before that I was in the army. That's when I met this gal from Louisiana. Beautiful gal. I was stationed right here at Fort Polk. We fell in love. She was a good lady. I wanted to marry her.

LUCIUS. Why didn't you?

MR. SIMONETTI. I don't know. I was only twenty at the time. Eventually I got transferred to Fort Dix in New Jersey, closer to my home. Never got back to Louisiana. After some time I got a letter from the lady tellin' me that she had a baby boy. Said it was mine. By then I was set to marry a girl back East.

(beat)

Time passed, we never had any children. She died a few years back of a stroke and I started thinkin' about the lady in Louisiana. I was lonely. I knew that I had a son somewhere and I decided it was time to come back and find him. My search brought me here.

LUCIUS. You're lyin'.

MR. TINKER. Lucius!

MR. SIMONETTI. Why do you say that?

LUCIUS. How old are you?

MR. SIMONETTI. Forty-three.

LUCIUS. I'm only fifteen. If you met her when you were twenty, how could I be your son. I'd have to be twenty-three or you'd have to be thirty-five. And if you were thirty-five then you don't look so good.

MR. SIMONETTI. *(nervously putting it together)* I said I was twenty when I met her, but I was in the army for ten years. Didn't I mention that?

MR. TINKER. No. I don't think that was how it was told. But don't worry, we can verify all this. If it's true, it'll all be documented somewhere.

*(From offstage we hear a scream. It's **WALRUS**. **RICARDO** runs onstage, and grabs **MR. TINKER**.)*

RICARDO. Mikey's lost. He was tryin' to swim out to the caves and he disappeared under the water. Walrus was tryin' to go after him but we pulled him back. You gotta come right now.

*(**RICARDO** and **TINKER** run off. **LUCIUS** stays put and stares off after the others.)*

*(MUSIC: **WHO ARE YOU (MIKE'S VERSE)**)*

*(Throughout the next monologue, **MIKE** is pulled on stage, his limp body being carefully placed on the dirt shore.)*

CALLAHAN. It took them almost two hours draggin' the lake before they found his body. By the time they got it up on the dirt, it was all swollen and blue. His eyes were wide open and I could swear I saw a smile on his face. He looked like they oughta put him in a jar with formaldehyde, like one of them frogs with the pins in 'em.

*(**LUCIUS** crosses to **WALRUS**, sitting on a rock, both fists in his mouth, sobbing. He touches his shoulder, but **WALRUS** brushes him off. He crosses back to **CALLAHAN**.)*

LUCIUS. *(to **CALLAHAN**)* Mike always said that some day he would swim out of here off to an island like the one with Jim Hawkins and Long John Silver. I believe he did. Now it's my turn.

(Music out)

(beat)

LUCIUS. You don't have to keep pretendin'. I know it's you.

CALLAHAN. How'd you figure it out?

LUCIUS. It wasn't hard.

CALLAHAN. Look, I gotta go. You wanna come with us, you're gonna have to run away. We'll be at the back fence tomorrow morning. We leave at seven a.m. Just tell Mr. Tinker this whole thing freaked me out. He'll buy it.

(He starts to exit.)

Sorry about your friend.

LUCIUS. What about Jim Hawkins? Is she okay with it?

CALLAHAN. It was her idea. Tomorrow morning. Seven a.m. Back fence. Pack light.

*(**MIKE** is carried off, followed by **TINKER** and the boys.)*

*(MUSIC IN: **THE BALLAD OF LIZARD**)*

There are moments in life that are defining moments, when you know that a decision or a choice you're making is gonna turn your whole world on its end. Taking Lizard with us...was one of those moments.

(The lights fade on the lake.)

SCENE 7

(On another area of the stage, lights up on **SALLY**, *packing the car. It is the next morning.)*

*(***CALLAHAN*** *enters from behind.)*

SALLY. And you don't think they recognized you?

CALLAHAN. No.

SALLY. But the kid recognized you, right?

CALLAHAN. Yeah. He's pretty smart, that one. He was right. He don't belong here.

(beat)

You should have seen that other kid when they pulled him outta the river. I ain't seen nothin' like that in my whole life.

SALLY. You sure you told him the right place 'n time?

CALLAHAN. Yeah, I told him.

*(***LUCIUS*** *enters, carrying his backpack and his box.)*

(MUSIC OUT)

(After a moment of silence where they all realize the gravity of the moment...)

(MUSIC IN: **YOU'RE GOIN' THERE TOO***)*

(During the next number the trio use suitcases and props to create a car and begin their journey. Most of this song takes place on the road. [wheels on trunks work great – but the imagination is limitless])

CALLAHAN. What's in the box?

LUCIUS. My skink.

SALLY. Your what?

LUCIUS. It's my lizard.

SALLY. Well, okay, I suppose he doesn't eat much.

LUCIUS. Where we headin'?

SALLY. *(to* **CALLAHAN***)* Cal didn't tell ya'?

CALLAHAN. I didn't have time.

LUCIUS. That your real name?

CALLAHAN. *(from the front seat)* No such thing as a "real" name, boy. It's all made up anyway.

SALLY. So he didn't tell you we're goin' to Alabama to do a play?

LUCIUS. No, ma'am. He said he was a shoe salesman from Brooklyn and that his wife had a stroke.

SALLY. I would imagine she would.

CALLAHAN. Lizard don't care much where we go, so long as we take him with us. Right, boy?

LUCIUS. Pretty much.

CALLAHAN. That's somethin' you can always count on, boy, life takes you with it, whether you want to go or not. Let's go!

*(He sings. MUSIC: **YOU'RE GOIN' THERE TOO**)*

*(**YOU'RE GOIN' THERE TOO**)*

IT JUST DON'T MATTER WHERE YOU'RE HEADED TO
DON'T MATTER IF IT'S EAST OR WEST
YOU'RE ALWAYS WINDIN' UP WHERE YOU'RE DOWN A FEW
DON'T MATTER WHAT
YOU GOTTA KEEP YOUR CARDS
CLOSE TO THE VEST

THERE'S LOTS OF STUFF TO TELL GOT LOTS OF GAS
GOT STORIES COMIN' OUT YOUR BUTT
BUT - YOU GOTTA TAKE A SHARP TURN DON'T MISS THE
     PASS
YOU THINK IT'S LEFT
OH SHIT, IT'S RIGHT, NOW YOU'RE FLAT ON YOUR ASS

BUT WHOEVER YOU ARE AND WHATEVER YOU DO
IT NEVER SEEMS TO CHANGE WHAT THIS WORLD PUTS YOU
     THROUGH
CAUSE IT REALLY DON'T MATTER IF IT'S ME OR IT'S YOU
LIFE SAYS WHEREVER I GO, YOU'RE GOIN' THERE TOO

SALLY. We're goin' to Birmingham, Alabama. Southside Repertory theatre. We're doin' a play about a ship-wreck and there's a great part for you.

CALLAHAN. We got another *Treasure Island* to do but then…

(**SALLY** *moans*)

…yeah, well, it's money and we need some.

SALLY. But after that it's Shakespeare's *The Tempest.*

LUCIUS. Who's Shakespeare?

SALLY. *(to* **CALLAHAN***)* There's your audience, Cal. You can make up your own words, he'll never know.

(*She sings:*)

DON'T MATTER WHAT YOU SAY, SOME FOLKS DON'T HEAR
    A WORD
YOU MIGHT AS WELL BE SPEAKIN' GREEK
IT COULD BE PROFOUND OR IT COULD BE ABSURD
ONE THING, YOU KNOW
YOU'LL ALWAYS GET ANOTHER SHOT NEXT WEEK

SALLY & CALLAHAN.

CAUSE WHOEVER YOU ARE AND WHATEVER YOU DO
IT NEVER SEEMS TO CHANGE WHAT THIS WORLD PUTS YOU
    THROUGH
CAUSE IT REALLY DON'T MATTER IF IT'S ME OR IT'S YOU
LIFE SAYS WHEREVER I GO, YOU'RE GOIN' THERE TOO

LUCIUS.

STOP!

CALLAHAN & SALLY.

THERE AIN'T NO STOPPIN' WHEN YOU'RE ON THIS ROAD

LUCIUS.

BUT!

CALLAHAN & SALLY.

BUT, DA, BA, DA, DEEBA NOT TODAY

LUCIUS.

I KNOW…

SALLY & CALLAHAN.

YOU'LL KNOW IT WHEN YOU SEE IT
AND YOU'LL SEE IT WHEN YOU KNOW
AIN'T NO USE IN TRYIN' TO FIGHT
WHAT'S GONNA HAPPEN ANYWAY

CALLAHAN.

YOU GOTTA ACT LIKE YOU'RE SOMEBODY

SALLY.

EVEN IF YOU'RE NOT

CAUSE LIFE'S ABOUT THE PART YOU PLAY

CALLAHAN.

IF YOU GOTTA TAKE A PISS

SALLY.

AND YOU AIN'T GOT NO POT

CALLAHAN.

YOU GOTTA TAKE YOUR SHOT

MARK YOUR SPOT

LUCIUS.

OR HOLD IT AND PRAY

ALL THREE.

CAUSE WHOEVER YOU ARE AND WHATEVER YOU DO

IT NEVER SEEMS TO CHANGE WHAT THIS WORLD PUTS YOU
THROUGH

CAUSE IT REALLY DON'T MATTER IF IT'S ME OR IT'S YOU

LIFE SAYS WHEREVER I GO, YOU'RE GOIN' THERE TOO

CALLAHAN. What's it say?

ALL THREE.

IT SAYS WHEREVER I GO, YOU'RE GOIN' THERE TOO

IT SAYS WHEREVER I GO, YOU'RE GOIN' THERE TOO

*(At the end of the number, the lights shift and we have
moved into the early evening.)*

SALLY. Cal, we ought to stop pretty soon and set up camp
before it gets too dark.

(Lights begin to flash on the car.)

SALLY. *(cont'd)* What's that? Cal, what is it?

LUCIUS. Looks like a police car.

SALLY. Maybe they're lookin' for Lizard?

CALLAHAN. Might just be a speed trap.

SALLY. But what if it's not? Should we try to run it?

CALLAHAN. I have a better idea. Both of you get in the back. Lizard, curl up there next to Sally. Sally, cover most of his body with that blanket. Make sure you cover his feet and hands.

(taking a leash out of the glove compartment)

Put Mac's old dog collar around his neck.

SALLY. *(confused)* What are you doin'?

CALLAHAN. Just trust me. Get in the back seat and do what I'm tellin' you to do.

*(**SALLY** and **LUCIUS** do what **CALLAHAN** says. They pull over and a couple of **COPS**, **HOMER** and **KNUTE**, come up with flashlights.)*

HOMER. Evenin', folks. Just a routine stop. We're lookin' for a runaway from Leesville State School. A deformed runaway. You couldn't miss 'em if you tried.

CALLAHAN. Haven't seen nobody like that, officer.

HOMER. Better check in the back, Knute.

CALLAHAN. Go ahead boys. Just my wife back there tendin' to our carsick dog.

*(The cop opens the back door and shines the light on **SALLY**.)*

KNUTE. How are you, ma'am. Sorry to disturb you.

SALLY. That's quite alright, officer.

KNUTE. *(looking in at **LUCIUS**)* Take a look here, Homer. That's the ugliest dog I've ever seen. What kind 'a dog is it?

CALLAHAN. Short-haired, tailless Weinerrheiner. Won best of breed at the Lake Charles show. That's where we're comin' back from.

KNUTE. No shit? Weinerrheiner? I never heard tell of that one 'fore. I'll be damned. Where'd you get 'em?

HOMER. *(laughing)* Why, you want one?

KNUTE. I might. My wife raises Pekingese. She'd get a kick out of this one.

CALLAHAN. Just give me a call if you're ever in Rosepine. Name's Simolinsky. I'm in the book.

KNUTE. Okay, I'm gonna take you up on that.

HOMER. *(laughing)* Let's go, Knute.

(beat)

You folks have a nice rest of your trip home. And if you see anything of that boy, give the police a call.

CALLAHAN. Will do, officer. Have a good night.

(As the cops start to leave, LUCIUS barks. CAL and SALLY look frightened, the COPS look back, surprised at first, and then they just laugh.)

(The COPS exit.)

LUCIUS. *(proud)* They really believed I was a dog.

CALLAHAN. Until you barked. What were you thinkin'?

LUCIUS. *(laughing)* I thought I sounded pretty good.

CALLAHAN. *(serious)* Yeah, well, from now on let me think and you just look like you look. That way we all stay outta trouble.

(They get out of the car and start to set up camp.)

CALLAHAN. *(cont'd)* Let's set up camp here tonight. Tomorrow morning Sally and I'll drive into Newllano to do our last *Treasure Island.* *(to LUCIUS)* You'll stay here. It's not a good idea for you to come with us. When we get back we'll take off for Birmingham, Alabama...and *The Tempest.*

(SALLY starts to set up sleeping bags and blankets.)

SALLY. Twinkies and chips tonight boys. But tomorrow we'll have rabbit.

CALLAHAN. We trap our own and cook 'em fresh. I'll set the traps first thing in the morning.

LUCIUS. Can I help you with the traps?

CALLAHAN. Yeah. You can come with me so you know where I put 'em. Then later on you gonna have to check 'em. Bring back whatever we catch. You won't have to skin'em or anything. Just bring them back here. And no barking, think you can do that?

LUCIUS. Sure.

(SALLY sits down next to LUCIUS and hands him a Twinkie. CALLAHAN starts to lay out his sleeping bag.)

CALLAHAN. I sure can't wait 'til we get to old Wanda's place.

SALLY. *(to LUCIUS)* Wanda runs the new repertory company.

CALLAHAN. Brand new building. Been renovating it all spring. This'll be the first show of their opening season.

SALLY. *(to LUCIUS)* And we're gettin' paid. Imagine that.

CALLAHAN. Then if you're any good, you can become a professional. Travel out to Hollywood and become a movie star.

LUCIUS. Yeah, I could be in *Lassie*.

CALLAHAN. You could BE Lassie.

LUCIUS. *(shy)* That's what I meant.

SALLY. Cal, that ain't nice.

LUCIUS. It's okay. I know what he means.

CALLAHAN. *(He recites to LUCIUS:)* "The fringed curtains of thine eyes advance, and say what thou seest yond."

SALLY. Eye.

CALLAHAN. What?

SALLY. "The fringed curtains of thine eye advance."

CALLAHAN. What did I say?

SALLY. Eyes, plural. It's only one eye.

CALLAHAN. I don't think anyone's gonna care if I say eyes instead of eye.

SALLY. The playwright might care.

CALLAHAN. It's Shakespeare, I don't think he'll be there.

SALLY. I'm only saying that...

CALLAHAN. What's the next line, cause now I have no idea what it is. You're throwin' me off track. And from now on, only correct me if I'm way off.

(SALLY shifts into bed mode. She climbs into her sleeping bag.)

SALLY. *(changing the subject)* Lucius Simms. You know what? You have the most beautiful colored eyes I ever did see.

(LUCIUS smiles, actually he blushes, and is speechless. CALLAHAN laughs.)

I'm serious. Have you seen the color of his eyes. *(to LUCIUS)* Your mom or your pop must have really beautiful eyes.

(beat)

Do you remember what your dad looked like?

LUCIUS. He died before I was born.

SALLY. What about your mom?

LUCIUS. Never met my mother. I lived with this woman who took me in. Never knew anybody else.

(SALLY motions to CAL to talk to LUCIUS.)

CALLAHAN. I didn't know that about your dad. If I'd a known he was dead I would've never pulled the Simonetti routine. Tinker showed me your records and it didn't say anything about your daddy being dead so I thought...

LUCIUS. What?

CALLAHAN. *(stalling)* Well, it just weren't complete, that's all. Look, Lizard this whole thing is a business deal.

SALLY. Cal!

CALLAHAN. Well, it is. We lost Jerry, the guy we originally cast. He's drying out at the V.A. in Galveston. He sucked anyway, but you're perfect. And we'll save money on makeup.

SALLY. Cal!

CALLAHAN. Well, that's what you said.

SALLY. I'm sorry, Lizard. He has no sense of propriety.

CALLAHAN. Look, Lizard, you learn your lines, take direction and get paid union wages. What's better'n that?

LUCIUS. How much of this is true?

CALLAHAN. Jesus, Lizard, what do I have to do?

(beat)

Okay, so Jerry's not in the hospital. He ougtta be but he's not. I just made that up for dramatic effect.

LUCIUS. What's that?

SALLY. Lyin'.

CALLAHAN. I was just tryin' to make a better story. No harm in that, is there? Can we just all go to bed and get some sleep. We have lots to do in the morning.

(CALLAHAN crawls in beside SALLY.)

SALLY. Good night, Lucius Simms. You're gonna be a great Caliban.

LUCIUS. Who's that?

SALLY. That's the character you're gonna play in *The Tempest.*

LUCIUS. Is he a good guy or a bad guy?

SALLY. Well, since you'll be playing him, I think he's gonna be a good guy.

(beat)

Good night. Sleep tight. Don't let anything bite you.

(LUCIUS watches as SALLY and CALLAHAN start to spoon.)

(He climbs up into a tree, looking down on CAL and SALLY. His mind is racing with adventure.)

*(MUSIC IN: **SET MY SPIRIT FREE** - Reprise)*

LUCIUS.
MY IMAGINATION'S ON FIRE
MY HEAD IS FULL OF PICTURES
AND MY HEART'S FULL OF DESIRE
AND I KNOW I WON'T SLEEP TONIGHT
CAUSE THE DREAM I'M DREAMIN' CAN'T COME TRUE
'TIL I SEE IT IN THE MORNING'S LIGHT

(The lights fade to shadowed night as we shift to the morning.)

*(MUSIC TRANSITION: **THE BALLAD OF LIZARD**)*

SCENE 8

(CALLAHAN addresses the audience. LUCIUS plays out the narrated journey.)

CALLAHAN. The next mornin' after Sally and I left for town, Lizard made his way along the path, following the map I made him best he could. He wandered into a peach orchard with pine trees and sweet gum for miles...until he came across what looked like an old pump house. Tin roof, broken windows, pine straw crammed into the cracks, along with some crushed up old milk cartons. That's when it happened.

(A black girl, RAIN [posing as a boy] in boots, cutoff jeans and a floppy hat appears behind LUCIUS. She has a bunch of rabbits strung together over her shoulder.)

RAIN. Freeze!

(LUCIUS freezes in place)

Turn around slow. I got a shotgun, so don't act funny.

(LUCIUS slowly turns around and sees RAIN, who clearly does not have a gun.)

LUCIUS. You don't got no gun.

RAIN. I didn't say I had it with me. I just said I got a gun, n' I do. It's in the house. Yonder, you can look for yourself. It's aimed right at your head, so don't be movin' too quick.

LUCIUS. If you just let me find what I'm lookin' for, I'll be on my way.

RAIN. And what might you be lookin' for, white boy? As if I didn't know. Who gave you permission to kill my rabbits?

LUCIUS. They're not your rabbits.

RAIN. *(yelling)* Shoot!

(LUCIUS ducks. Nothing happens. RAIN laughs uncontrollably.)

They are my rabbits. Just like the ground you're standin' on. It all belonged to my Great Grand Daddy, Chief Running Dear. He was a Creek warrior. That makes me half Creek, so don't try anything funny.

LUCIUS. Is that gun in there loaded?

RAIN. I'd be pretty stupid if I said no?

LUCIUS. So is it?

RAIN. *(laughing)* No!

>*(beat)*

>You hungry?

LUCIUS. Why?

RAIN. Cause I'm fixin' on eatin' some lunch.

>**(RAIN** *starts off towards the pump house. She stops and looks back.)*

>*(shy-like)* Are ya comin'?

>**(LUCIUS** *moves towards her. She excitedly races into the house and starts to shed her hunting clothes, and make herself more "girl-like." She watches to see if he's following, peeks out the window to make sure he's still there.)*

RAIN. *(cont'd) (from inside)* We don't get many visitors around here.

LUCIUS. Do you live here alone?

RAIN. Most of the time.

>*(beat)*

>What about you? Where do you live?

LUCIUS. *(lying)* Oh, I'm an actor. All my life. We mostly live on the road. On my way to Birmingham to do a play right now.

RAIN. *(from the house)* Really? That's so excitin'!

>**(RAIN** *enters from the house with a tray of bowls (rabbit stew). Her hair is down and she's clearly wearing her best dress. She is quite pretty.)*

>**(LUCIUS** *sees her and is speechless.)*

What's the name of it?

LUCIUS. The name of what?

RAIN. The play you're doin' in Birmingham.

LUCIUS. *(caught)* Oh. The magician and the slave.

RAIN. Sounds nice. I wish I could see your play.

LUCIUS. That would be great.

> *(beat)*

> Are you really Creek?

RAIN. Let's say that I'm what I look like, and I'm something
else that you can't see

> *(RAIN hands LUCIUS a bowl of stew.)*

> Go on, try it.

LUCIUS. What is it?

RAIN. Rabbit stew. Mama's best recipe.

LUCIUS. That who lives here with you?

RAIN. No. Mama's dead. She died two years ago in a flash
flood. Stream jumped its banks. We never found her.

> *(LUCIUS tries the stew. He's skeptical at first, but once he
> tastes it he can't get enough.)*

LUCIUS. It's great.

> *(beat)*

> My daddy died before I was born.

RAIN. What's your mamma like?

LUCIUS. Ain't ever had a mamma.

RAIN. I didn't think you could do that, not have a mamma.

LUCIUS. Do you have a daddy?

RAIN. No.

LUCIUS. Well, that's not supposed to be possible either.

RAIN. Mamma always said that some things weren't meant
to be understood, just believed.

> *(As the two of them chow down, a voice pierces the air
> from within the woods.)*

> *(PREACHER JONES, a tall, lanky black man, with a
> dark manner and a pensive stare, enters from the clear-
> ing and calls out to RAIN. He is clearly drunk.)*

PREACHER. *(laughing and slurring)* Rain! That your mama's rabbit stew I'm smellin'? I got me an appitite needs fillin' so you'd best be ready for me.

(**RAIN**'s *whole manner changes. She grabs the bowls and throws them into the house. She grabs a sack and pulls* **LUCIUS** *up off the ground.*)

RAIN. Come on, Lizard. I wanna show you something.

PREACHER. Rain! You hearin' me girl?

LUCIUS. Who's that?

RAIN. Don't matter. Come on.

PREACHER. Rain! Come on out here girl!

(MUSIC: Intro to **THE SILVER BOWL.***)*

(**RAIN** *and* **LUCIUS** *climb to a spot where they begin to lower themselves down into a cave.*)

(**RAIN** *crawls in snug against the side of the cave. She is out of breath and clearly nervous.*)

LUCIUS. Who was that?

RAIN. This half-blind Preacher snake. Comes here every two weeks or so and he...

LUCIUS. What?

RAIN. He gives me letters from my Aunt Eunice in Detroit. I'm gonna go live with her someday.

LUCIUS. This preacher...

RAIN. He ain't really a preacher. He was Mama's boyfriend a long time ago, and he says he's got papers to show that I belong to him. He's what they call a guardian.

LUCIUS. What's that mean, a guardian?

RAIN. Means he can come out here drunk whenever he wants, beat me and have his way with me.

LUCIUS. Why don't you run away?

RAIN. I tried. But they just send me back. N' then it's worse. But I got a plan. Look!

(**RAIN** *reaches into her bag and pulls out a silver bowl. She puts it on a rock, as though placing it on an altar.*)

LUCIUS. Wow! That's beautiful. What is it?

RAIN. This silver bowl came from my Grandpa Running Deer. It's my most precious possession. My mama left it to me. Someday I'm gonna run far away from here. I'm gonna take this bowl, sell it and use the money to get me to Detroit.

(beat)

This bowl...it holds magic.

(RAIN *takes out a flask and pours some liquid into the bowl.)*

*(MUSIC IN: **THE SILVER BOWL**)*

LUCIUS. What's that?

RAIN. Just ordinary water. But somethin' happens to it when you pour it into the bowl. Just do like I do.

(RAIN *pours the water into the bowl and begins to sing.)*

(THE SILVER BOWL)

DRINK FROM THE SILVER BOWL
IT WILL HEAL YOUR HEART AND CLEANSE YOUR SOUL
IT MAKES ALL THINGS PURE AND ALL THINGS WHOLE
LIKE THEY WERE BEFORE AND FOREVER MORE

*(She takes the bowl, drinks and hands it to **LUCIUS**.)*

RAIN. *(cont'd)* Now you.

(LUCIUS *takes the bowl, swirls it like **RAIN** did and sings with her.)*

RAIN & LUCIUS.

DRINK FROM THE SILVER BOWL
IT WILL HEAL YOUR HEART AND CLEANSE YOUR SOUL
IT MAKES ALL THINGS PURE AND ALL THINGS WHOLE
LIKE THEY WERE BEFORE AND FOREVER MORE

LUCIUS. You believe that?

RAIN. I sure do. In the Bible it tells us that it's done to us as we believe.

LUCIUS. The Bible says that.

RAIN. Accordin' to my mama it does. I drink this water whenever Preacher comes around. It cleans my insides, washes him away.

(MUSIC SEGUES from **THE SILVER BOWL** *to* **WHATEVER I DID KNOW***)*

LUCIUS.

(WHATEVER I DID KNOW)

WOULDN'T IT BE GOOD IF SOMEONE KNEW
ONE DRINK AND THEY'D LOOK PERFECT JUST LIKE YOU
WOULDN'T IT BE GOOD TO KNOW THAT MAGIC COULD BE
   REAL

RAIN. There's nothin' wrong with how you look. You look just fine.

LUCIUS. You think?

RAIN. I do.

(She reaches out and touches his face.)

I think you're beautiful.

(LUCIUS *stares into her eyes and smiles. She reaches in and kisses him softly on the lips. [It's important that this moment is innocent in nature])*

LUCIUS.

WOULDN'T IT BE GOOD IF TIME STOOD STILL
ONE WISH AND YOU'D STAY JUST THAT WAY UNTIL
I WAS READY TO UNDERSTAND THESE THINGS I FEEL

RAIN. If you could be anything in the whole world what would you be?

LUCIUS. You mean like a wish?

RAIN. No! Mama said that wishes weren't as strong as knowin'. What could you KNOW about yourself?

LUCIUS. *(sings)*

IF I COULD BE MOST ANYTHING
I THINK I'D CHOOSE ME A FOREST KING
MY CASTLE INSIDE A TALL OAK TREE
I'D CLIMB, THIS TIME
I'D CLIMB WAY UP TO THE TOP AND SING

MY VOICE WOULD FLY THROUGH THE CLOUDS ON WING
AND I WOULDN'T CARE WHAT WENT ON DOWN THERE
    BELOW
IF I COULD BE WHATEVER I DID KNOW

What about you? When you get outta here.

What're you gonna know?

RAIN.

IF I COULD REACH INSIDE MY MIND
IT MIGHT BE SCARY WHAT I MIGHT FIND
A LIGHT SO BRIGHT
THAT THE WORLD WOULD BE AGLOW
AND SO

I'D FORCE THE DARK FAR AWAY FROM ME
AND LIGHT THE WAY FOR US ALL TO SEE
AND IT WOULDN'T MATTER WHEREVER WE MAY GO
IF I COULD BE WHATEVER I DID KNOW

RAIN & LUCIUS.

I WOULDN'T HAVE TO CARE WHAT THE WORLD HAD TO SAY
NO MATTER WHAT THEY'D SAY I'D KNOW
THAT THERE'S SOMETHIN' INSIDE ME BIGGER THAN THE
    SKY
I'D FIND MY VOICE WITHIN THE CROWD
AND YELL MY NAME SO DAMNED LOUD
THEY'D HEAR ME CLEAR UPON THE MOON
AND SOON I WOULD SEE WHAT I SHOULD BE
NOT SHOULD BUT COULD THEN I WILL BE FREE
TO BUILD CASTLES INSIDE OF TALL OAK TREES AND THEN
WHEN I'M SITTING TALL I'LL SHOW
TO EVERYONE BELOW I'LL CROW
THAT I CAN BE WHATEVER I CAN KNOW
YES I WILL BE WHATEVER I DID KNOW

(**LUCIUS** *grabs the bowl and holds it out to* **RAIN**.)

(*She takes hold of it and the two of them drink together.*)

(*The* **PREACHER** *appears in the entrance to the cave.
MUSIC OUT. NOTE: this moment is intentionally chill-
ing.*)

PREACHER. *(looking in on the two of them)* What the hell do we have here? Looks like the circus must be in town. You found yourself your own little freak show.

RAIN. He's not a freak. Don't say that. His name is Lizard. He's an actor.

PREACHER. I see. So that's what it is. You got a mask on boy?

LUCIUS. No, sir.

PREACHER. Them your real eyes?

LUCIUS. Yes, sir.

RAIN. There's rabbit stew back at the house.

PREACHER. Yeah, you both been eatin' it. Since when do I pay for other people to be eatin' my food?

LUCIUS. I'm sorry...

PREACHER. Don't you speak when you're not bein' spoke to. You ate my food and now you're touchin' my property.

RAIN. He wasn't touchin' me...

(The PREACHER reaches in and grabs RAIN, pulling her to him forcibly.)

PREACHER. You're my property and nobody touches you but me. Let's go.

(The PREACHER throws RAIN to the other side of his body, clearly making it impossible for LUCIUS to leave the cave without passing him. In an instant, he reaches across to LUCIUS and pulls him up off his feet and drags him out of the cave and back to the house.)

(RAIN runs back and gathers up her sack. She notices LUCIUS's backpack as well, and moves the bowl to his bag.)

PREACHER. *(cont'd)* Rain! Come on, we don't want to be inhospitable to our guest.

*(MUSIC: **THE BALLAD OF LIZARD**.)*

(The PREACHER drags LUCIUS back to the pump house with RAIN following.)

(**CALLAHAN** *appears, [in one of his many disguises].
He approaches* **LUCIUS**, *who breaks free and runs into*
CALLAHAN'*s arms.*)

CALLAHAN. Now where you been all this time, boy? You
were supposed to be out picking berries for your mamma's pie.

PREACHER. This here your boy?

CALLAHAN. Sure is. He's been gone all day. We was worried
sick about him.

PREACHER. You ought be teachin' him some manners. He
was takin' advantage of my little girl here.

RAIN. That ain't true.

PREACHER. Rain! Get in the house. Now!

(**RAIN** *starts into the house. She crosses to* **LUCIUS** *and
gives him his bag.*)

(*There is something odd about the way she hands him
the bag, as if she wants to say something but can't.*)

RAIN. Goodbye.

(**RAIN** *exits into the house.*)

PREACHER. I want you both off 'a my property and never to
come back, hear? If you do, I'll make sure you don't
never leave.

CALLAHAN. Oh, we understand. Not a problem here, sir.
You have a nice night, now.

(*MUSIC IN:* **SAVE HER**)

(*The* **PREACHER** *enters the pump house as* **CALLAHAN**
and **LUCIUS** *make their way back into the woods.*)

SCENE 9

LUCIUS. *(holding* **CALLAHAN** *back)* What're we gonna do. We can't just leave her there.

CALLAHAN. What are you talkin' about?

LUCIUS. We gotta go back there and take her with us.

CALLAHAN. What we have to do is get to the truck and get outta here before he calls the authorities and reports what he saw.

*(**CALLAHAN** starts off. **LUCIUS** follows.)*

LUCIUS. But he's gonna hurt her. I know it.

CALLAHAN. Did you hear what he said?

LUCIUS. I don't care what he said.

CALLAHAN. Well, I do. Now let's go.

LUCIUS. Where are we?

CALLAHAN. Doesn't matter.

LUCIUS. *(yelling)* YES IT DOES. WHERE ARE WE?

CALLAHAN. Twelve miles east of Newllano.

LUCIUS. I have to come back here tomorrow.

CALLAHAN. *(grabbing* **LUCIUS***)* We ain't comin' anywhere near this place tomorrow and that's that. Now let's go, I'm done talkin'.

*(**CALLAHAN** has made his way to **SALLY** and the truck.)*

LUCIUS. I'm not goin' with you.

SALLY. What's the matter?

CALLAHAN. Kid got into some trouble with a black girl and her father.

LUCIUS. He's not her father.

CALLAHAN. I don't care who he is.

LUCIUS. He has his way with her. She told me.

SALLY. What? Who's he talking about?

CALLAHAN. It doesn't matter. All that matters is that people know we're here and we have to get outta here. Now let's go.

LUCIUS. No.

CALLAHAN. *(to* **LUCIUS***)* Look, I don't care what you got yourself involved in. It ain't my business. My business is gettin' us to Birmingham where we got jobs waitin' for us. Frankly, nothin' else matters. Got it?

LUCIUS. No, I don't got it!

> *(SAVE HER)*
>
> I CAN'T JUST DISAPPEAR
> I CAN'T JUST LET HER STAY THERE
> HE'LL HURT HER IF WE LET HIM HAVE HIS WAY
>
> I CAN'T JUST STAND HERE BLIND
> PRETEND SHE DOESN'T MATTER
> EVERYONE MATTERS, DON'T THEY

CALLAHAN.

> THINGS AREN'T ALWAYS WHAT THEY SEEM

LUCIUS.

> BUT YOU WEREN'T THERE YOU DIDN'T SEE
> IF YOU HAD SEEN HER FACE
> OR TOUCHED HER SKIN YOU'D FEEL THE SAME AS ME

SALLY. *(spoken)* Lucius...

LUCIUS.

> I WON'T JUST WALK AWAY
> SOMEONE HAS GOT TO SAVE HER
> I WON'T KNOW IT ANY OTHER WAY

CALLAHAN.

> IT AIN'T OUR BUSINESS WHAT'S BEEN GOIN' ON
> GOT NO INVESTMENT IN THEM FOLK
> AS FAR AS I'M CONCERNED WE'RE GONE
> SO GRAB YOUR THINGS AND LET'S BE ON OUR WAY
> AIN'T NOTHIN' HERE TO CHANGE MY MIND
> NOTHIN' YOU CAN DO OR SAY
> CAN SAVE HER
> NO ONE CAN SAVE HER
> PEOPLE DO WHAT THEY PLEASE
> AND THEY DON'T GIVE A SHIT
> KNOCK YOU DOWN TO YOUR KNEES
> THEN YOU'RE COVERED IN SPIT

JUST DON'T GET IN THEIR WAY
THAT'S THE LESSON TO LEARN
CAUSE IT'S ALWAYS THE SAME
AND YOU'LL PAY IN RETURN IF YOU
SAVE HER
YOU CANNOT SAVE HER
YOU CAN ONLY EVER SAVE YOURSELF

LUCIUS. Do you really believe that?

CALLAHAN. I have to believe that. No other way to believe in this world.

SALLY. Cal, maybe we could find someplace to hide the truck and see what we can do.

CALLAHAN. We can't do anything! You know that.

(to **LUCIUS***)*

What do you think'll happen if they find us, huh? You think they'll just take you back and let us go on our merry way? No!

(to **SALLY***)*

We'll go to jail. And I'm not willin' to risk that for some people I never even met.

LUCIUS. Well I am!

I CAN'T JUST WALK AWAY

*(***CALLAHAN** *grabs his bags and turns to* **LUCIUS***.)*

CALLAHAN. Fine. Where's them traps?

LUCIUS. Here, in my bag.

*(***CALLAHAN** *opens* **LUCIUS** *'s bag and pulls out the traps, followed by the silver bowl. He throws it to* **LUCIUS***.)*

CALLAHAN. You wanna tell us about this.

LUCIUS. It's Rain's.

CALLAHAN. You stole it?

LUCIUS. No. She must've put it in there.

CALLAHAN. Jesus Christ! He's gonna come lookin' for this.

SALLY. Who? Who's gonna come looking for this?

CALLAHAN. Pack it all up. Now! We're leavin'!

(to **SALLY***)*

Sally, let's go.

LUCIUS. I'm not leavin' her there alone.

CALLAHAN. You do what you like.

(to **SALLY***)*

We're leavin'.

SALLY. Cal, we can't just leave him here.

CALLAHAN. It's his decision.

(to Sally)

I knew this was a bad idea. Why do I listen to you?

*(***CALLAHAN*** takes off.* **LUCIUS** *stands stunned, holding the silver bowl.)*

LUCIUS. *(to* **SALLY***)* I didn't steal it. Honest. I didn't know it was in there. Rain must've put it in there.

SALLY. Why would she put this bowl in your bag?

LUCIUS. She said it was her most precious possession, that it was her way out.

SALLY. Look Lizard, I know Cal. He's gonna leave here with you or without you. There's nothing you can do. Let's just go and you and I can figure this out later.

LUCIUS. I can't.

(Beat: **SALLY** *doesn't know what to do.)*

SALLY. Alright. Goodbye, Lucius Simms. You would have made one helluva Caliban.

*(***SALLY*** exits.* **LUCIUS** *stands holding the bowl. He remembers something* **RAIN** *said.* **RAIN** *appears in a pool of light.)*

RAIN. This silver bowl came from my Grandpa Running Deer. It's my most precious possession. My mama left it to me. Someday I'm gonna run far away from here. I'm gonna take this bowl, sell it and use the money to get me to Detroit.

(beat)

This bowl...it holds magic.

RAIN. *(cont.)*

> DRINK FROM THE SILVER BOWL
> IT WILL HEAL YOUR HEART AND CLEANSE YOUR SOUL

RAIN & LUCIUS.

> IT MAKES ALL THINGS PURE AND ALL THINGS WHOLE
> LIKE THEY WERE BEFORE...AND FOREVERMORE

> *(***CALLAHAN*** returns. He and* **LUCIUS** *lock eyes. In a flash,* **LUCIUS** *grabs his bag, stuffs the bowl inside and crosses to* **CALLAHAN**.*)*

LUCIUS. I know why she put the bowl in my bag.

> *(***LUCIUS*** runs ahead of* **CALLAHAN** *to catch up with* **SALLY.** **CALLAHAN** *looks around, makes sure no one has followed and exits.)*

END ACT I

ACT 2

SCENE 1

*(In the darkness we hear a harmonica version of **THE BALLAD OF LIZARD**.)*

(Lights slowly fade up on a ransacked room, clearly in the middle of being reconstructed.)

(A Chinese restaurant/theatre. **CALLAHAN**, **SALLY** *and* **LIZARD** *enter.)*

*(**CALLAHAN** looks around, he is not happy.)*

CALLAHAN. What the hell is this?

SALLY. Are you sure it's the right place?

LIZARD. *(reading the sign)* "The Golden Palace!"

CALLAHAN. *(calling out)* Wanda! Wanda, you here?

(From behind the stage we hear a voice: strong, full and excited.)

WANDA. *(off stage)* Cal? Is that you?

CALLAHAN. We're out here.

*(**WANDA** enters. A Texan tornado, she enters with a gust of energy that takes our breath away.)*

WANDA. Cal! I can't believe you finally made it. *(big hug)* I was beginning to think I was gonna have to play all these roles myself.

(yelling offstage)

Everyone, come on out here and meet our star!

(to **SALLY***)* You must be Sally.

(to **LIZARD***)* And you must be...

67

CALLAHAN. Lucius, but you can call him Lizard.

WANDA. *(looking at him)* What happened to you, boy? Accident?

LIZARD. No. I think God did this on purpose.

WANDA. He does have a wicked sense of humor sometimes.

CALLAHAN. So, where's the theatre?

WANDA. This is the theatre.

(beat, looking at **LIZARD***)*

I thought you said his name was Jerry.

LIZARD. Lucius, Lucius Simms.

WANDA. So where's Jerry Koswinski?

CALLAHAN. Forget about Jerry, what do you mean THIS is the theatre?

WANDA. I mean, this is the theatre.

SALLY. The Golden Palace?

WANDA. Yeah, it used to be a Chinese restaurant. This was the kitchen.

CALLAHAN. Wanda, how the hell do you expect to turn this place into a theatre in...

WANDA. *(looking out into the house)* Eddie, remind me to get rid of those meat hooks.

CALLAHAN. Wanda, what were you thinkin'? You asked me to come out here and do a season of regional theatre. Real theatre! How the hell do you think we're gonna turn this pit into...

WANDA. You nervous, Cal? Don't be nervous.

*(MUSIC IN: **JUST IMAGINE**)*

I'm the director. Let ME be nervous, okay? Let us not forget that THIS is not the play. This is merely the PHYSICAL SPACE where the play takes place. The real play is in the mind, the imagination...

(She sings.)

(JUST IMAGINE)

CLOSE YOUR EYES AND JUST IMAGINE
THOUGH IT'S ROUGH AND UNREFINED
THIS SPOT IS ONE OF A KIND

AND THE MOMENT I SET FOOT HERE
I KNEW THAT I WAS PUT HERE
TO TURN THIS SPACE INTO THE PLACE
I'VE ALWAYS CONJURED IN MY MIND

*(**WANDA** summons her workers to join her in convincing **CALLAHAN**.)*

WANDA & COMPANY.

JUST IMAGINE OPENING NIGHT
JUST HEAR THE BUZZ IN THE AIR
THE PRAYER THAT IT'LL BE RIGHT
JUST IMAGINE OPENING NIGHT
SOMEONE FUSSING WITH HAIR
SOMEONE ADJUSTING THE LIGHT

AND WHATEVER IT TAKES WE'LL GET THERE
AND WHATEVER THE STAKES WE ALL SHARE
AND WE'LL WORK THROUGH THE ACHES
EVERY BACK THAT IT BREAKS
ALL THE NERVES AND THE SHAKES
AND THE STUPID MISTAKES
AND IT'S ALL FOR THE SAKES OF THE PLAY
AND OPENING NIGHT

LIZARD. You sure are optimistic.

WANDA. No other way to be.

(As she sings the next verse, the stage begins to be transformed into the set for The Tempest *(albeit rustic in nature). Costumes are tried on **CALLAHAN**, **SALLY** and **LIZARD**, with the company acting out the rehearsal process.)*

WANDA & COMPANY.

CLOSE YOUR EYES AND JUST IMAGINE
LAY SOME CARPET, SLAP SOME PAINT
FOR THE FAINT OF HEART IT AIN'T

WANDA & COMPANY.

> BUT I SAW IT AND WAS CERTAIN
> BUILD A STAGE AND HANG A CURTAIN
> SOME SWEAT, SOME TEARS
> KNOCK BACK SOME BEERS
> AND TURN THIS BITCH INTO A SAINT
>
> JUST IMAGINE OPENING NIGHT
> JUST SEE THE LINE OUT THE DOOR
> IT'S SUCH A BEAUTIFUL SIGHT
>
> JUST IMAGINE OPENING NIGHT
> THE CHAMPAGNE'S READY TO POUR
> THE CAST AS HIGH AS A KITE
>
> THERE'S STILL PLENTY TO BEG AND BORROW
> BEFORE BREAKING A LEG TOMORROW
> RIGHT NOW WE'RE GATHERING PROPS
> AT LOCAL PAWN SHOPS AND SWAPS
> SLATHERING MOPS AFTER PAINTING THE DROPS
> AND NONE OF IT STOPS TILL WE HEAR
> PLACES ARE CALLED

EDDIE. Places!

WANDA. Just Imagine!

EVERYONE.

> JUST IMAGINE, JUST IMAGINE, JUST IMAGINE
> OPENING NIGHT

> *(When the song ends, everyone is costumed and staring out at the audience.)*

> *(**WANDA** starts to applaud.)*

WANDA. It's going to be brilliant. I can feel it.

> *(to **CALLAHAN**)*

> Can't you feel it?

CALLAHAN. You don't wanna know what I'm feeling.

WANDA. We are gonna give Birmingham the best "Tempest" they've ever seen. And I am predicting that we will run well past our first week.

SALLY. Wait a minute, it's a six-week run, right?

WANDA. Well, not exactly.

CALLAHAN. What do you mean, not exactly?

WANDA. Didn't you get my note?

CALLAHAN. Now that's a lousy line. You should never ask people who've driven seven hundred miles to get here, slept on the ground, borrowed money for gas, almost got themselves arrested - you should never say to these people, "Didn't you get my note?"

WANDA. So you didn't?

LIZARD. What did it say?

WANDA. We can't do the season as planned. We only have enough money to get us to the first performance of *The Tempest.* After that, it's up to the audiences.

CALLAHAN. Meaning?

WANDA. Meaning if we have one we'll play. If not, we're done.

SALLY. But you promised us six months of repertory at Equity pay.

CALLAHAN. *The Tempest, Uncle Vanya,* that Tom Stoppard piece, *The Texas Trilogy...*

WANDA. We lost our grant. Government's drying up.

CALLAHAN. Jesus, Wanda. Help me understand this. I haven't gotten paid to act in two years. You know what I do for a living? I unload plumbing supply trucks, part time. At least I did. I borrowed three hundred dollars to get here. From my Aunt, Wanda! She's eighty-six years old. Got rheumatoid arthritis and lives in public housing in Houston - where they kill people for less than what you've done to me!

(beat)

So you're tellin' me there isn't any season at Equity pay? There isn't any season at all? Just *The Tempest?*

WANDA. Which might not run past opening night.

CALLAHAN. Jesus Christ!

> *(beat)*

What time are rehearsals?

WANDA. That a boy! Tomorrow morning, nine o'clock sharp. We'll be blocking the entire first act.

CALLAHAN. We WILL get paid for *The Tempest?*

WANDA. What kind of business do you think we're running here? Of course you'll get paid.

> *(**CALLAHAN** storms out of the room, followed by **SALLY** and **LIZARD**.)*

> *(calling after him)*

I just hope to God you have your lines learned, and the way Shakespeare wrote 'em.

> *(beat)*

Alright everyone, back to work.

> *(The lights shift and we are in the hotel room.)*

SCENE 2

(CAL enters the room changing into a dress shirt. **SALLY** *and* **LIZARD** *follow in after.)*

CALLAHAN. I can't believe she did this to me. And she just figured I'd "deal" with it. Just like everything else I have to "deal" with in my life.

SALLY. Calm down, Cal, I'm sure she's not happy about it any more than you are.

LIZARD. Where's the bathroom?

CALLAHAN. Down the hall.

(LIZARD exits to the bathroom.)

(CALLAHAN starts to put his wallet and change in his pockets. He's clearly going out.)

SALLY. Where you goin'?

CALLAHAN. Down to the bar for a drink. You wanna come?

SALLY. We have rehearsal tomorrow morning at nine. Why don't we turn in early and...

CALLAHAN. I need to relax a little bit, okay?

SALLY. But you've been doin' so good.

CALLAHAN. What am I, a little boy? I'm not Lizard.

SALLY. I know.

CALLAHAN. Then don't talk to me like that.

SALLY. I'm sorry. That's not what I meant.

CALLAHAN. I'm goin' down for one drink, for Christ's sake.

SALLY. You're just gonna get more upset about this whole thing.

CALLAHAN. I'll be fine. I just need to unwind.

SALLY. Look, you came out here to be an actor. Drinking interferes with your acting.

CALLAHAN. What does that mean? I haven't had an acting job in over two years.

SALLY. Yeah, that's what I'm talkin' about.

CALLAHAN. What? You sayin' I haven't been tryin' to get any work?

SALLY. That's not what I'm sayin'.

CALLAHAN. You think I get a kick out of unloading plumbing supplies? You know what acting's like. It's not so easy breakin' in.

SALLY. You're over forty. Cal, you're not breakin' in any more.

CALLAHAN. Hell I'm not.

(beat)

You don't think I'm any good, do you?

SALLY. I never said that. I just think that if you're so serious about your acting, getting drunk the night before your first rehearsal isn't such a good idea.

*(**CALLAHAN** starts to exit.)*

SALLY. *(cont'd)* Cal, I'm askin you not to go.

CALLAHAN *exits past* **LIZARD** *as he enters from the bathroom.*

LIZARD. Where's he goin'?

SALLY. Down to the bar.

(beat)

You hungry?

LIZARD. No.

SALLY. Me either. Funny how that works. Things fall apart and we lose our appetite. All those people tryin' to lose weight. They outta have the fallin' apart diet.

LIZARD. I'll sleep out here on the floor.

*(**LIZARD** starts to unpack his bag and lay out his sleeping gear. He takes out the silver bowl and puts it next to his pillow.)*

SALLY. Tell me about your silver bowl.

LIZARD. It's not mine.

SALLY. I know. Cal told me about the preacher...

LIZARD. It's not the preacher's either. And I didn't steal it. I know Cal thinks I stole it, but I didn't.

SALLY. I didn't think you did. I was just interested in the story, that's all.

LIZARD. *(beat)* What does it mean when somebody says, "He has his way with me?"

SALLY. Well, if a woman says it about a man it can mean that he's forcin' her to have sex with him.

*(**LIZARD** turns away, upset. **SALLY** steps behind him and touches his shoulder.)*

Rain's a lucky girl to have a friend like you, Lucius. There's nothing you can do right now. You know that, don't you?

*(**LIZARD** hasn't said a word. He stares straight ahead. **SALLY** starts to turn away...)*

LIZARD. You ever get a feelin' so deep down that you don't know what to call it 'cause you've never felt quite this way before?

*(MUSIC IN: **MISSING MYSELF**)*

SALLY. You missing Rain?

LIZARD. I don't know. Maybe. It's just...whoever I thought I was doesn't make sense to me any more and I don't know who's here in his place - and I miss the knowin', you know?

SALLY. *(smiling)* I do know.

(MISSING MYSELF)

AS CHILDREN WE ALL PLAY WITH TOYS
DOLLS AND HORSES, GIRLS AND BOYS
PRINCES, KINGS AND FROGS AND WIZARDS
FLYING HORSES, SNAKES AND LIZARDS

FILL OUR MINDS WITH MAGIC POTIONS
SOARING OVER TURQUOISE OCEANS
WE MAKE UP STORIES 'BOUT TOMORROW
FILLED WITH GLORIES, NEVER SORROW

OH, TO GO THERE AGAIN
OH, TO KNOW WHERE AGAIN
I MIGHT FIND ME
THERE RIGHT BEHIND ME I'LL BE

SALLY. *(cont.)*

> LOST, TOSSED AWAY
> ON A SHELF
> TIL ONE DAY
> YOU WAKE UP AND YOU SAY
> I'M MISSIN' MYSELF

LIZARD. Yeah, it's like somethin' I always knew was there isn't there any more and what I always thought I was lookin' for, doesn't seem important any more.

SALLY. And that kind of puts you nowhere, don't it?

LIZARD. Except for this silver bowl, which is the only thing I can think about.

> *(beat)*

SALLY. Do me a favor, Lucius? Go downstairs and check on Cal before he tells too many lies and pretends to be someone he's not. Make sure he doesn't get into too much trouble.

LIZARD. How'm I supposed to do that?

SALLY. Just go down and be with him. That ougtta do it.

LIZARD. Okay.

> *(He starts to exit and turns back.)*

Sally, Cal's a lucky guy to have a friend like you. You and me, we're a lot alike.

SALLY. I don't look like no Lizard, now get outta here. And don't you come back without him.

> *(**SALLY** shoos **LIZARD** off and starts to get ready for bed.)*

> YOU COME INTO THIS WORLD A CRYIN'
> YOU GROW YOUR WINGS THEN TAKE OFF FLYIN'
> AND THEN ONE DAY YOU'RE BROUGHT TO SCHOOLS
> YOU'RE TAUGHT TO FOLLOW PLANS AND RULES
>
> YOU MAKE SOME CHOICES TAKE SOME CHANCES
> YOU ROLL THE DICE YOU DANCE THE DANCES
> THE MUSIC STOPS THE CHAIRS ARE TAKEN
> THE GAME IS DONE YOUR HEART IS BREAKIN'

OH, TO GO THERE AGAIN
OH, TO KNOW WHERE AGAIN
I MIGHT FIND ME
THERE RIGHT BEHIND ME I'LL BE

LOST, TOSSED AWAY
ON A SHELF
TIL ONE DAY
YOU WAKE UP AND YOU SAY
I'M MISSIN' MYSELF
I'M MISSIN' MYSELF

(The lights fade on **SALLY** *as she stares ahead, searching…)*

SCENE 3

*(MUSIC IN: **EVERYBODY NEEDS SHOES** - Reprise.)*

*(Lights up on the bar. **CALLAHAN** is putting the moves on a woman, **RHONDA**, standing against the wall of the bar.)*

*(**LIZARD** enters and watches.)*

CALLAHAN. *(singing)*
I GOT FOUR INCH STILETTOES
FISH NETS AND SUCH
NYLONS AND SILK HOSE
SO NICE TO THE TOUCH
OH I KNOW WHERE YOU'RE ACHIN'
YOU GOT NOTHIN' TO LOSE
COME TO ME, I'M THE MAN, OH YEAH
EVERY BABY NEEDS SHOES

*(He sees **LIZARD** and pulls him up to the table, trying to get him to dance with him. **LIZARD** awkwardly joins him.)*

CALLAHAN. *(cont'd)* Lizard! Hey! My boy. Come on up here. Rhonda, this here's my boy.

*(**CALLAHAN** crosses to **LIZARD** and brings him over to the table, where **RHONDA** has just sat down.)*

Lizard, this is Rhonda. She's a...well she's a...friend of mine.

*(to **RHONDA**)*

Whattya think of him, huh? Unique, right?

*(**RHONDA** doesn't know what to make of **LIZARD**. She tries to size him up but she is extremely drunk so she blurts out more than she means to.)*

RHONDA. What the hell happened to him?

CALLAHAN. Nothin' happened to him. This is how he was born. Came out this way. And let me tell you somethin' you don't find natural talent like this every day.

RHONDA. Ohhhh...he's adorable. *(to* **LIZARD***)* Your dad here's quite the salesman.

*(***CALLAHAN** *starts laughing when she calls him his dad.)*

LIZARD. He's not my dad.

RHONDA. Really? Cause I can see the resemblance.

CALLAHAN. *(practically choking with laughter)* You don't say?

(He starts to kiss her.)

Let's see if you can taste the resemblance.

(He kisses her hard and then pushes her towards **LIZARD.***)*

Now try him. See if there's any resemblance?

*(***RHONDA** *grabs* **LIZARD** *and pulls him towards her. He pulls away.)*

Go on, son, give her a try. It won't cost you nothin'.

*(***LIZARD** *pulls away and runs into the arms of the* **BARTENDER,** *who is on his way over to* **CALLAHAN***'s table. He's carrying a bat. Rhonda exits to the ladies room.)*

BARTENDER. *(to* **LIZARD***)* Why don't ya tell your old man that when her husband gets back he'd better be at another table.

LIZARD. He's not my old man.

BARTENDER. She causes trouble here every week. I don't even bother callin' the cops any more. I just swing the bat and whoever it cracks...oh well!

(beat)

Just thought you'd wanna know.

*(***LIZARD** *crosses back to* **CALLAHAN,** *who is alone at the table.)*

LIZARD. The bartender says you oughta leave before her husband gets back.

CALLAHAN. Tell him to mind his own goddamned business. We're only havin' a drink, for Christ's sake.

LIZARD. He's got a bat.

CALLAHAN. I got a bat, too. Bet mine's bigger.

(He laughs.)

CALLAHAN. What, did Sally send you down here to check up on me?

LIZARD. It's late. We should all be gettin' to bed. Rehearsal's first thing in the morning.

CALLAHAN. *(angry)* I know what time rehearsal is. I don't need you to tell me.

(RHONDA enters from the ladies room.)

RHONDA. Do I look all freshened up?

CALLAHAN. I don't know. Ask your husband.

RHONDA. Is he back?

CALLAHAN. Not yet, so we'd better get a move on if we want to make anything out of tonight.

(He grabs RHONDA and kisses her passionately on the mouth. She pulls away.)

RHONDA. I just put on new lipstick. Don't!

(LIZARD tries to pull CALLAHAN away.)

LIZARD. Come on, Cal, let's go upstairs.

(CALLAHAN pushes him to the floor. He regrets it instantly.)

CALLAHAN. *(going to him)* I didn't mean to do that. I'm sorry.

LIZARD. You're drunk.

CALLAHAN. Yeah, you oughta try it sometime. Things don't look so bad. Even you, you don't look so ugly after a few drinks.

LIZARD. *(trying to take him away)* Why don't we go back to the hotel room.

(CALLAHAN, in a burst of energy, takes hold of LIZARD.)

CALLAHAN. You know somethin' Lizard? I gotta tell you somethin. You're not too bright. I mean, you are bright, sort of, but you're gullible.

LIZARD. What's that mean?

CALLAHAN. You swallow a lot of stuff that shouldn't ever go down. You believe people. And most people lie. Like that woman the guy from the school was talkin' about. That Tinker guy, he was talkin' about some woman who raised you.

LIZARD. You mean Miss Cooley.

CALLAHAN. *(laughing)* Now right there. You see, that's the problem. You call her Miss Cooley. Why would you call your mamma Miss Cooley? Unless you believed all that bunk about you not having a mamma.

*(**LIZARD** realizes what he's just said and almost throws up.)*

You gonna tell me now that you didn't know she was your mamma? Cause I find that hard to believe. You see, that's what I mean by gullible. You gotta grow up, be a man. It's time for you to stop bein' so stupid. No way you're gonna survive if you keep pretendin' that the world's a good place. It ain't.

LIZARD. I don't believe you. I don't know why you're tellin' me these things, but I don't believe you. You're just drunk. Miss Cooley's not my mamma. She was never married before.

CALLAHAN. *(laughing)* No, I don't believe she was.

*(**LIZARD** starts to leave. **CALLAHAN** crosses after him. **RHONDA** steps in.)*

RHONDA. Hey, come on, leave him alone. Come on back to the party.

*(**CALLAHAN** pushes her away. The **BARTENDER** hits the bat against the wall.)*

BARTENDER. That's it, pal, get out of here.

*(**LIZARD**, who has stopped at the door, watches as **CALLAHAN** walks towards him.)*

CALLAHAN. Oh yeah, one more thing. Your father's not dead either.

(**LIZARD** *pushes him against a wall and jumps back.*)

LIZARD. Shut up! I don't believe you.

CALLAHAN. You can believe what you want. He's alive.

LIZARD. No, I don't believe you.

(*MUSIC IN:* ***BLUE SKIES***)

(**LIZARD** *runs away from* **CALLAHAN**.)

(*The lights fade as* **CALLAHAN** *steps into a pool of light and addresses the audience.*)

CALLAHAN. Lizard didn't want to believe that his Father was still alive or that Miss Cooley was his mother. If she was, how come she never told him? How come she put him in a home and lied about his Daddy bein' dead? That's a lot for a boy to think on.

(*beat*)

I wasn't sure why I told him at that exact moment. I'd been thinkin' about tellin' him. I guess it was the booze. That was somethin' for me to think on.

(*beat*)

We didn't talk that night when I got back to the room. Lizard was pretendin' to be asleep. He and Sally got pretty good at that, pretendin'! And by the time I woke up the next morning he was already gone. Sally said he'd gone lookin' for someone to buy the silver bowl.

SCENE 4

(Lights shift, as a man appears on a bench. **LIZARD** *paces in front of him.)*

*(***ROBERT HOWELL** *is a museum director, well spoken, kind, intuitive. He takes* **LIZARD** *immediately into his conscious care.)*

HOWELL. *(to* **LIZARD***)* Waiting for someone?

(beat)

Are you lost? You've been waiting out here an awful long time.

LIZARD. I'm waiting for the museum to open.

HOWELL. That makes sense. It's almost time, isn't it.

*(***HOWELL** *gets up, takes out a set of keys and begins opening up the museum.)*

LIZARD. Do you work here?

HOWELL. Might say I work here. Though some would argue with you about that. But I suppose there's some truth to it.

(beat)

We're early yet. Officially the place doesn't open 'til ten, but I like seeing the paintings first thing in the morning, when they're fresh and rested from the night before. Come on in.

*(***HOWELL** *and* **LIZARD** *enter the museum.)*

LIZARD. I never thought of paintings resting before. I guess that makes sense.

HOWELL. Everything makes sense to someone. That's what makes this world such a wonderful place to live in.

LIZARD. It ain't so wonderful in some places.

HOWELL. Sure it is. You bring your mind wherever you go and if it's wonderful in your mind then it's wonderful in the place.

LIZARD. That's a strange way of lookin' at it.

HOWELL. Only way I see works.

(He stops in front of a painting.)

Take this painting. What do you see?

LIZARD. A girl and her mamma.

HOWELL. *(smiling to himself)* Have a seat.

*(**LIZARD** sits in front of the painting.)*

Every painting in this room was rescued from the ruins of Germany in World War Two. All of them saved from being destroyed.

LIZARD. Are you the museum director?

HOWELL. *(as if remembering it)* Why yes! Robert Howell. And you are?

LIZARD. Lizard Simms.

HOWELL. Good to meet you Lizard.

(beat)

What was I saying?

LIZARD. The war.

HOWELL. Yes, the war. When the war was coming to an end, I'd been sent to rescue these pieces of art. I'll never forget the light in those German cities after the armies surrendered. There was a suspension of dust in the air with shafts of light pouring through, as if God had had enough and was forcing himself through the rage. The things I saw, bodies brutalized, cities leveled to the ground, swollen corpses in the streets.

(beat)

Then I came across this painting, somehow untouched by the ravages of war. It was clearly the work of a master.

LIZARD. This one here?

HOWELL. *(describing what he is looking at)* A woman servant in fresh linen, standing before a window, braiding her daughter's hair. Do you see their expression?

LIZARD. I think so.

HOWELL. What would you call it?

LIZARD. Happy.

HOWELL. Hopeful. Right then in the midst of all that was wrong with the world I knew with absolute certainty that there was life on the other side of this one. So I gave up my disillusionment with the world and its wars and I simply started over with that in my mind.

(pointing to the painting)

I take that hope everywhere I go.

(beat)

So what're you hopin' for?

LIZARD. I'm sorry?

HOWELL. Why are you here, other than to listen to me wax poetic?

LIZARD. *(remembering)* Oh! I have something I want to show you. It's a silver bowl that belongs to a friend of mine.

*(MUSIC IN: **THE SILVER BOWL**)*

*(**LIZARD** looks around for his backpack and realizes that he's left it on the bench.)*

Oh no, I left it outside on the bench.

(He races from the museum back to the bench. It's gone.)

No! I can't of lost it. It's her only hope.

*(**HOWELL** has followed him out to the street.)*

HOWELL. Who's only hope?

*(**LIZARD** is crushed.)*

LIZARD. Don't matter now. She was dependin' on me and now I've let her down.

HOWELL. It'll turn up. You'll see. It'll work out.

LIZARD. It ain't a painting. It's real. She's a real person and she needed me. Everything doesn't always work out.

HOWELL. Sure it does.

LIZARD. No. It doesn't.

> *(beat)*

Thanks for showin' me your painting.

> *(**LIZARD** walks away, leaving **HOWELL** in a pool of light, looking after him.)*

> *(The scene shifts from the street to the theatre.)*

SCENE 5

(A rehearsal for The Tempest.*)*

*(MUSIC IN: **A TEMPEST IN THE AIR**)*

(Like a Greek chorus, the acting company take their places to begin rehearsing a musical prologue.)

(A dramatic flourish of lights and fog are accompanied by the menacing music as the company create an ocean shipwreck.)

(Thunder and Lightning.)

*(**WANDA** appears in the midst of it all.)*

WANDA. Straight forward to the audience. Let them feel what you feel. You are caught in the midst of a terrible storm. Your lives are at stake. All of Earth is being swallowed up.

(to the booth)

Otto! More lightning! ALL of EARTH for Christ's sake, not just Birmingham...EARTH.

(massive lightning)

Thank you.

(beat)

Company! Go!

COMPANY.

(A TEMPEST IN THE AIR)

THERE'S A TEMPEST BREWING, A STORM IS STEWING
ALL HAD BEST BEWARE

AS THE SEAS KEEP SWELLING, THERE ARE CURSES YELLING
ALL HAD BEST PREPARE

IT'S A DEMON'S SQUALL THAT MAY NEVER STOP
CRASHING O'ER THE TOP OF THE MAST
HOLD FAST, OR YOU'LL ALL BE CAST
TO THE TEMPEST IN THE AIR

SHIPMASTER. Boatswain!

BOATSWAIN. Here, master, what cheer?

WANDA. *(to the* **BOATSWAIN***)* Get rid of the word cheer. There's nothing cheerful about this.

BOATSWAIN. Here, master, what...up?

WANDA. Good!

SHIPMASTER. Speak to the mariners. Fall to 't ya rely, or we run ourselves aground; bestir, bestir.

COMPANY.

THERE'S A TEMPEST RAGING, A SORC'RER STAGING
TRAITORS FATES FAREWELL

(TOLL THE BELL)

HIS REVENGE IS YEARNING, THEIR ETERNAL BURNING
IN THE GATES OF HELL

(IT'S FINAL KNELL)

HE WILL TAKE THEM DOWN TO THE BRINY DEEP
FOR THEIR FINAL SLEEP
FOR THERE'S N'ERE A PRAYER FOR A SOUL HE'LL SPARE
TO THE TEMPEST IN THE AIR

BOATSWAIN. Down with the top-mast; yare; lower, lower. Bring her to try with main-course.

(a cry from the others)

A plague upon this howling!

*(***CALLAHAN*** enters, confused.)*

CALLAHAN. What the hell is this?

WANDA. *(coming down the aisle)* It's the prologue, Cal.

CALLAHAN. Why are they singing it?

WANDA. Calm Down, Cal. It's just an idea I had.

CALLAHAN. A bad idea.

WANDA. Otto! *(lights come up)* Musicals sell, Cal. So we add a few numbers, sing a couple of songs...

CALLAHAN. You can't just add songs to Shakespeare.

WANDA. They had songs in their day.

CALLAHAN. Music, they had music. They didn't sing prologues.

WANDA. How to you know? Were you there?

SALLY. *(to* **CAL***)* Why don't we just try it and see what happens.

CALLAHAN. Are you kidding me?

*(***LIZARD** *enters holding his script.)*

And where the hell've you been?

LIZARD. I had some business I had to...

CALLAHAN. The only business you have is what I give you. Now get over here and let's rehearse. Singing is over, let's do some real acting.

WANDA. Alright everyone, let's take it from where we were before Prospero needed a drink.

(to **CALLAHAN***)*

And if you need to storm out of here again, I'll play the damn role myself.

(to the **COMPANY***)*

Take it from, "Thou poisonous slave..."

*(***CALLAHAN** *throws his script aside and takes his place onstage.)*

CALLAHAN. Can we run it with lights? I'd like to get an idea of what the HELL it's gonna feel like on opening night.

WANDA. It's gonna feel like this, but with less people.

(yelling to the booth)

LIGHTS!

(to **LIZARD***)*

Lizard! Off book, boy. If you need a line just call for it and someone will yell it out to you.

(The lights fade. **CALLAHAN***, now as Prospero, appears.)*

CALLAHAN. "Thou poisonous slave, got by the devil himself, upon thy wicked dam, come forth!

(There is a pause as everyone waits for **LIZARD** *to enter.)*

CALLAHAN. *(cont'd) (yelling off-stage)* That was your cue!

LIZARD. *(entering)* I wasn't sure.

CALLAHAN. I just said COME FORTH. How hard is it for you to remember a directive like that?

LIZARD. I wasn't sure if you were acting or practicing. So I didn't know if you really wanted me to enter.

CALLAHAN. YES! I want you to enter.

LIZARD. "As wicked dew as e'er my mother brushed from raven's feather from unwholesome fen, drop on you both. A southwest blow on ye, and blister ye all over."

CALLAHAN. "For this be sure, that tonight you will have cramps."

WANDA. *(yelling)* "THOU SHALT have cramps! Not YOU WILL...THOU SHALT."

CALLAHAN. "Side stitches that shall pen your breath up."

WANDA. "THY breath up! Not YOUR...THY!" Don't go getting colloquial on me.

CALLAHAN. This from the woman who put a song at the top of THE TEMPEST!

WANDA. Moving on!

CALLAHAN. "Side stitches that shall pen THY breath."

WANDA. That's where you hit him, Cal. Didn't you write this down when we blocked it? Someone throw Prospero his script.

CALLAHAN. I got it.

(CALLAHAN steps into LIZARD and hits him [we should know that it is both hard and an unconscious mistake]. He knocks him to the floor. LIZARD falls with a thud. CAL reaches out to make sure he's alright.)

CALLAHAN. *(cont'd)* You okay?

(LIZARD gets up and realizes that his mouth is bleeding. CALLAHAN steps in and tries to help him but LIZARD pushes him away.)

(CALLAHAN follows LIZARD off.)

(WANDA throws up her hands and calls the company back to the opening.)

WANDA. Oh, Mother of God in heaven above...alright everyone. Let's try that opening again.

*(MUSIC IN: **A TEMPEST IN THE AIR - Reprise**)*

(As the actors get in place for the prologue, **SALLY** *exits
off after* **CALLAHAN** *and* **LIZARD**.*)*

(The scene shifts to the dressing room.)

SCENE 6

(**LIZARD** *enters followed by* **CALLAHAN**.

(*The staging of the Prologue continues - in slow motion and shadowed*)

CALLAHAN. Look, I'm sorry. I didn't mean to hit you so hard.

LIZARD. That wasn't Prospero that hit me out there, it was you.

CALLAHAN. Come on, Lizard. You're just pissed off because you don't think I should've been with that woman last night, right? We were just havin' some drinks. Sally doesn't care.

LIZARD. I don't either.

CALLAHAN. We were just havin' some fun.

LIZARD. What about all that stuff about Miss Cooley and my Daddy bein' alive? Was that just you havin' some fun too?

(**SALLY** *enters.*)

SALLY. (*to* **CALLAHAN**) I think you owe Lizard an apology, Cal.

CALLAHAN. For what? I already said I was sorry I hit him so hard.

SALLY. He told me what you said to him last night.

CALLAHAN. Oh, come on. I was practically passed out. I barely remember what you're talkin' about.

SALLY. (*to* **LIZARD**) Tell him what he said.

CALLAHAN. (*to* **LIZARD**) Yeah, go on, tell me. Cause I'm sure what I told you was the truth. Not like that cock-and-bull story about a black girl who's really an Indian and that silver bowl that's supposed to belong to her mamma. I bet you took that bowl just to have some-thin' to remember her by.

(**LIZARD** *lunges at* **CALLAHAN** *and the two of them fall to the floor.*)

LIZARD. I'm gonna kill you. You bastard! I'm not a liar. I'm not like you.

(**SALLY** *steps in and breaks them up.*)

SALLY. That's enough. Enough! Lizard, what's wrong with you?

LIZARD. Somebody stole the silver bowl. That's what's wrong with me. Rain's dependin' on me and I let 'er down. That's what's wrong with me.

CALLAHAN. Yeah, well that's how the world works. You steal from somebody and then somebody steals from you.

LIZARD. I DIDN'T STEAL IT!

CALLAHAN. Everybody lets everybody down at some point, right Sally?

SALLY. Shut up, Cal. You don't know what you're talkin' about.

LIZARD. (*to* **CALLAHAN**) Is it true, what you said? Is Miss Cooley my mother?

CALLAHAN. Yeah, it's on your birth certificate.

LIZARD. And my father?

CALLAHAN. There were two boxes next to the word father, living and deceased, living was checked. No name, just the box checked.

(*beat*)

I mean, why'd you think he was dead in the first place?

LIZARD. Miss Cooley told me so.

CALLAHAN. Yeah, right, so it was up to her to tell you he wasn't really dead. Not me.

SALLY. That's the first smart thing you said all day.

(*to* **LIZARD**)

Lizard, take a walk.

(**LIZARD** *exits the room.*)

What is goin' on, Cal? What's this all about?

CALLAHAN. Look, you're the one who wanted to bring him with us.

SALLY. Yeah, but not to make his life worse than it was.

CALLAHAN. We should have never taken him. He was a mistake.

SALLY. He's not the mistake. You are! He knows who he is. And it doesn't have anything to do with names on a birth certificate. That boy has goodness written all over him. What do you have written all over you, Cal? Do you even know?

(**CALLAHAN** *stares ahead, nothing to say.*)

(*beat*)

I thought it was gonna be different this time, Cal. I really did. But it's not. It never is.

(**SALLY** *shakes her head and exits.*)

(*Lights fade to a pool of light on* **CALLAHAN**.)

(**LIZARD** *enters into his own pool of light as the lights shift to the museum.*)

SCENE 7

(**LIZARD** *sits in front of a painting and examines it.*
HOWELL *enters.*)

HOWELL. Usually when I find myself in front of this painting I need to be reminded of something.

LIZARD. I was just lookin' in the mamma's eyes.

HOWELL. What are you finding?

LIZARD. She really loves that little girl. I don't think she
would ever let anything happen to her.

HOWELL. No, I don't think she would.

(holding up **LIZARD**'*s bag)* By the way, would this be what
you were lookin' for the other day?

(**LIZARD** *runs over to him and grabs the bag, immediately pulling out the silver bowl.*)

LIZARD. You found it! Thank you.

HOWELL. Don't thank me. One of my workers found it on
the bench and brought it inside. We just didn't know
how to get in touch with you.

LIZARD. *(speeding through)* Mr. Howell, that girl who owns
the bowl, she needs me to sell it for her. How much is
it worth and would you be willing to buy it from me so
that I can send the money to her Aunt and she can get
her away from that Preacher?

HOWELL. Hold on, hold on. It's a beautiful bowl and I
wouldn't be surprised if you could get maybe ten dollars for it but...

LIZARD. Ten dollars? But it's silver.

HOWELL. No, it's not.

LIZARD. Sure it is. What else could it be?

HOWELL. It seems to be leaded glass with a hard lacquer
finish. They give these bowls away at carnivals and
county fairs.

(**LIZARD** *walks away and sits down on the ground, putting his head in his hands.*)

LIZARD. There's nothin' more I can do.

HOWELL. Now I don't believe that and neither should you. If everyone went around believing that there was nothing left to do, we'd all be walkin' backwards.

*(MUSIC IN: **AND SO IT IS**)*

HOWELL. *(cont'd)* You just have to reach inside your head and see what you can pull out. You'll be surprised how many answers you'll find in there.

LIZARD. This is different.

HOWELL. Not it's not. It's all the same. Only difference is the way some people look at it.

(*AND SO IT IS*)

ONCE THERE WAS A MAN
WHO LONGED TO SAIL THE SEA
THOUGH NO ONE EVER HAD BEFORE
HIS ONLY THOUGHT WAS, WHY NOT ME
AND SO HE BUILT A BOAT
THE FIRST ONE OF ITS KIND
EXACTLY HOW HE SAW IT IN HIS MIND

ONCE THERE WAS A MAN
WHO DREAMED THAT HE COULD FLY
HE NEVER QUESTIONED HOW HE WOULD
HE NEVER STOPPED TO WONDER WHY
HE MADE A PAIR OF WINGS
AND JUMPED INTO THE BLUE
HE KNEW HE HAD TO MAKE HIS DREAM COME TRUE

SEE IT, DREAM IT, UNTIL YOU KNOW
TAKE IT, MAKE IT, UNTIL IT'S SO
AND SO IT IS

ONCE THERE WAS A MAN
A MAN LIKE YOU AND ME
HE WANTED MORE THAN WHAT HE SAW
HE HEARD A VOICE THAT SET HIM FREE
IT SAID THE WORLD IS GOOD
IT SAID THAT YOU SHOULD KNOW
YOU'RE PART OF EVERYTHING THAT MAKES IT GROW

DOESN'T MATTER WHAT YOUR TAUGHT
OR WHAT YOU'VE LEARNED
YOU CAN FLY, YOU CAN SOAR
DOESN'T MATTER THAT IT'S NEVER BEEN DONE BEFORE
IT JUST TAKES ONE, TO OPEN THE DOOR

ONCE THERE WAS A MAN
MIGHT AS WELL BE YOU
BUILD YOUR BOAT AND MAKE YOUR WINGS
DREAM THE THINGS YOU WANT TO COME TRUE
LET YOUR SOUL REMEMBER WHO YOU ARE
THERE IS NOTHING TOO HIGH
NOTHING TOO FAR

IF YOU CAN SEE IT, DREAM IT
UNTIL YOU KNOW
TAKE IT, MAKE IT
UNTIL IT'S SO
AND SO IT IS
AND SO IT IS
AND SO IT IS

HOWELL. *(cont'd)* Nothing is ever the end of anything. It's always the beginning of *something else.* You remember that and you think about your friend again and see what other ideas you come up with.

(**LIZARD** *exits.* **HOWELL** *crosses down to the painting and stares at it. A smile crosses his face as the lights fade.)*

SCENE 8

(Backstage of the theatre, opening night.)

(The cast is assembled, listening to **WANDA.***)*

WANDA. Alright everyone, listen up. The play is at a very delicate stage. It could be half decent or it could embarrass us for the rest of our lives. But regardless, it's going on in fifteen minutes so a couple of things...

(to **CALLAHAN***)*

Prospero, if you blow that last speech again I'll kill you. Got it.

(to the men)

Singing sailors, remember, you think you're about to die, so act scared for Christ's sake. It's a hurricane, not the tornado from *The Wizard of Oz.*

(to the booth)

Ronnie, where was the follow spot on Arial's big scene?

RONNIE. I'm saving it. The gels have been melting and this one's got to last.

WANDA. Yeah, well, it might only have to last through tonight. And if that spot doesn't follow her your check is gonna bounce all over this state.

(to **MIRANDA***)*

Miranda, I noticed a very suspicious glint under the lights today.

MIRANDA. Daddy said I'd have to keep it in.

WANDA. *(trying to stay calm)* I told your Daddy last night, and I told your orthodontist this morning, the retainer comes out. And if it's not out tonight, you won't need it anyway, 'cause you won't have a tooth left to retain. How many times do I have to tell you, there weren't any orthodontists on this island. That's why it was PARADISE!

CALLAHAN. So when do we get paid?

WANDA. You can all pick up your checks tomorrow morning. After that we split the house, if there is one. The review will be on my desk by midnight. We'll know at the party if there's going to be a tomorrow.

(Everyone starts to walk away.)

CALLAHAN. *(to WANDA)* How's the house?

WANDA. Maybe there'll be some late shows. They're rewiring the light board. Soldering and everything. The whole place stinks. Sometimes I wonder why we do this.

(big smile)

Because we LOVE IT, right?

(WANDA exits.)

(MUSIC IN: A TEMPEST IN THE AIR)

(Lights come up on a dressing room, SALLY is helping put makeup on LIZARD.)

SALLY. You and Cal talking?

LIZARD. I'm not Lizard right now, I'm Caliban.

SALLY. Sorry. Wow! You really seem so calm. I'm amazed. Me, I'm all butterflies and nerves.

LIZARD. I'm gonna throw up.

(LIZARD finds a trash can and starts to heave.)

SALLY. That's more like it.

(The actors perform the opening musical number while SALLY and LIZARD continue.)

LIZARD. I don't think I can go out there.

SALLY. You have to. Otherwise the whole show'll come to a halt.

WANDA. *(running in)* Ariel, what the hell are you doing in here. You're on.

SALLY. He's throwing up.

WANDA. Who's not throwing up. Go!

(SALLY exits.)

WANDA. *(cont'd)* You're gonna be alright.

LIZARD. I don't know.

WANDA. That wasn't a question. Now pull it together and get out there. You're the best actor we got. You know that don't you?

(LIZARD doesn't know if she's telling him the truth)

Incredible natural talent. That's what you got. Go out there and use it. It's a gift, what you can do. Go give 'em your gift. Break a leg.

LIZARD. You too.

WANDA. Hope not.

(MUSIC OUT: Sound effects continue throughout the scene)

(The prologue concludes and lights come up on the play itself.)

(WANDA watches as CALLAHAN makes his entrance as Prospero. He is visibly nervous. He clears his throat and starts to speak... nothing. He does it again... nothing.)

(LIZARD enters the scene and prompts him.)

LIZARD. "...thou shalt pinch me as thick as honeycomb, each pinch more stinging than bees that made 'em. Aye?"

(CALLAHAN is clearly lost. He stares at LIZARD, who motions him that it is his turn to talk.)

CALLAHAN. "Thou most lying slave..."

(This isn't the line LIZARD is looking for. He lets CALLAHAN know that it's the wrong line. He does this as subtly as possible. CALLAHAN just repeats the line again.)

CALLAHAN. *(cont'd)* "Thou most lying slave..."

(CALLAHAN starts waving his arms in LIZARD's direction as if to deflect the attention off himself.)

*(**LIZARD** mimics him and starts waving his arms. Finally...**SALLY** steps in and attempts to save the moment.)*

SALLY. *(stepping into the light)* "Abhorred slave...

*(**LIZARD** almost collapses in relief at the sound of **SALLY**'s voice.)*

...therefore wast thou deservedly confined into this rock, who hadst deserved more than a prison."

*(**LIZARD**, so excited that **SALLY** had saved the scene, turns to **CALLAHAN**, who he is sure will now remember his line. Instead...)*

CALLAHAN. "Thou most lying slave..."

*(**CALLAHAN** and **LIZARD** start to circle one another.)*

CALLAHAN. *(cont'd)* "Thou most lying slave..."

*(**LIZARD** doesn't know what to do so he just starts talking, no dialect or heightened word. He just makes it up.)*

LIZARD. *(beat)* So this is how you repay me. I took you all over the island. I showed you where the herons nested, where the deer drank at the stream. And everywhere we went you named things for me. And I learned to speak. Sometimes you or Miranda sang. And soon I even knew words for things I'd never seen. Like love..

CALLAHAN. *(pulled in)* "Poisonous wretch."

LIZARD. All night I tried to sleep but the words kept getting jumbled up in my head. I could think but I didn't know whether thinking was a blessing or a curse because all I could think about was love.

(beat)

But what good was knowing the word for love when I could never know the thing itself.

CALLAHAN. *(regaining his footing)* Go to work before I tell Ariel to pinch you to death.

LIZARD. But what about my lessons?

CALLAHAN. You know too much for your own good already.

LIZARD. But the names of the seasons, you haven't told me yet.

CALLAHAN. What for? It's wasted on you. You are as dense as a swamp.

LIZARD. And the stars. You were going to tell me about the stars.

(LIZARD waits for an answer. CALLAHAN just stares at him. They stand there staring into one another's eyes. The moment is just about to get unbearably uncomfortable when CALLAHAN jumps forward, remembering his way FINALLY!)

CALLAHAN. Hagseed, hence! Fetch us in fuel. And be quick...

(The entire company, in the wings, applauds.)

(A pool of light comes up on CALLAHAN.)

And like a record player that had been turned up from 33 to 45, the play was up to speed again.

(The lights shift to indicate time change.)

The second act was less eventful. Nobody was REALLY horrible, just the usual. And I really thought the few people who made it through the night seemed to enjoy it. That or they were just happy it was finally over. I know I was.

*(MUSIC IN: **A TEMPEST IN THE AIR**)*

(The cast lines up for their curtain call. They bow.)

(After the bow the actors turn the stage into Wanda's house, the opening night party.)

CALLAHAN. *(cont'd)* Once everyone got to Wanda's house it wasn't long before she read the review.

*(**WANDA** appears in a pool of light.)*

WANDA. "The most riveting performance in Southside Repertory Company's production of *The Tempest*, was turned in last night by a lighting cable that overheated and threatened to burst into flame midway through the second act."

(beat)

The rest of it's not so good. On the bright side, we save money by having the opening and closing night party all on the same night.

(The party starts to break up as the lights shift.)

SCENE 9

(CALLAHAN appears in the hotel room. He's getting dressed to leave. LIZARD enters.)

LIZARD. Sally said you were leavin'.

CALLAHAN. That's right.

LIZARD. Where you goin'?

CALLAHAN. I have some ideas.

LIZARD. I'm sorry about the show.

CALLAHAN. What're you sorry about? You were great. In fact, if it weren't for you, I'd still be out there sayin' "Thou most lying slave." I don't know. Maybe my dreams need some reshapin'.

(CALLAHAN starts down the steps to the street. LIZARD follows.)

Wanda told me she asked you to stay with her. She thinks you're a pretty good actor. That's not such a bad idea, you know. You could start over, make new friends.

LIZARD. But I have old friends that need me.

CALLAHAN. Yeah. I know.

(CALLAHAN starts bringing the trunks onstage. SALLY enters.)

SALLY. So, what's the verdict?

CALLAHAN. It hasn't come up yet.

SALLY. Lizard, Cal has an idea he'd like to run by you.

CALLAHAN. *(to LIZARD)* Look, Lizard, I'm sorry about the way I've been. About the bowl and the girl and all. What's her name.

LIZARD. Rain.

CALLAHAN. Rain, yeah. I'm sorry.

(beat)

You wanna go back there and get her?

LIZARD. Really?

CALLAHAN. Yeah, provided we can still find the spot.

LIZARD. It's twelve miles east of Newllano. Don't you remember clocking it?

CALLAHAN. Sort of.

SALLY. So it's settled then.

*(**CALLAHAN** and **LIZARD** start putting the car back together.)*

*(MUSIC IN: **YOU'RE GOIN' THERE TOO**)*

You both go back to Louisiana, I'll take care of my business and we'll all meet up somewhere down the road a bit.

CALLAHAN. Okay by me. Lizard?

LIZARD. Okay by me.

*(**CAL** and **LIZARD** set up the car.)*

SALLY. *(to **LIZARD**)* You just have to promise me to keep an eye on Cal. Feed him his lines when he needs 'em.

CALLAHAN. I won't need any feedin' thanks.

*(taking **SALLY** in his arms)*

See you soon.

*(**SALLY** and **CAL** kiss.)*

(Lights shift to the car. The trip is underway.)

SCENE 10

LIZARD. What'll we do when we get there?

CALLAHAN. We'll kidnap Rain 'n take her with us.

LIZARD. But what about the Preacher?

CALLAHAN. No preacher ever stopped me from doin' anything.

LIZARD. What about Sally? Is she really gonna meet up with us or is she leavin' for good?

CALLAHAN. Now see that's the thing about Sally. When she says she's gonna meet up with you, you can set your watch by it.

LIZARD. So you two are okay?

CALLAHAN. Sure. We're always okay.

(SFX: Thunder storm and rain.)

(They stop the car and look forward.)

(to **LIZARD***)*

I'd like to see that preacher's face when he comes back and she's gone.

(They get out of the car, taking it apart and stashing it away.)

LIZARD. He beats her.

CALLAHAN. I know.

LIZARD. And he has his way with her.

CALLAHAN. He won't never do that again. We'll see to that.

(beat)

This spot look familiar?

LIZARD. Not really.

CALLAHAN. Well let's just head on in. Keep about a hundred feet apart, and whoever sees the stream first, yell.

*(***CALLAHAN** *and* **LIZARD** *split up.)*

*(***CALLAHAN** *canvasses the entire stage while narrating.)*

CALLAHAN. *(cont'd)* We came out of the orchard and into the pine trees just when the rain completely stopped. The air was cooler here, like I'd remembered from before. We followed a path the water had cut down the hill.

(beat)

Beyond the weeds stood the pump house. The door flapped open and shut. I looked inside, there was nothin' to speak of. No signs that anyone had ever lived here. Place smelled like a fire had gone out a long, long time ago.

*(**LIZARD** makes his way to the pump house and runs in.)*

LIZARD. *(yelling)* Rain! Rain, we come back.

*(**CALLAHAN** steps out from behind the tree.)*

CALLAHAN. There's nobody here.

LIZARD. We come back too late. I knew it. Somethin's wrong. Somethin's terrible wrong.

(starting to cry)

It's my fault. He didn't like her runnin' off with me.

CALLAHAN. Now you don't know that. Come on, let's get back to the truck.

LIZARD. I know it. I can feel it in my bones.

*(**LIZARD** starts to hyperventilate.)*

CALLAHAN. Okay, okay.

(beat)

I got me an idea. Let's go.

*(The lights shift and we are back at the truck. **CALLAHAN** pulls out a suitcase and rummages through for some clothes. He pulls out the Simonetti clothes and one of Sally's dresses.)*

CALLAHAN. *(throwing **LIZARD** the dress)* Put this on.

LIZARD. Why?

CALLAHAN. We're goin' to the courthouse. Findin' us a preacher.

*(MUSIC IN: **YOU'RE GOIN' THERE TOO**)*

*(While **LIZARD** and **CALLAHAN** continue to dress, the stage is transformed into the Beauregard Parish courthouse.)*

SCENE 11

*(A **WOMAN** sits behind a desk. She is in conversation
with **HOMER**, the cop from the road. The **WOMAN** looks
up and addresses **CALLAHAN**.)*

WOMAN. What can I do for you folks?

CALLAHAN. Just some information that would make me the
happiest man in the world.

HOMER. Rest room's down the corridor past the automo-
bile tags.

CALLAHAN. I'm afraid you misunderstand. This is my fian-
cee', Miss Sarah Wills. And I'm Rudy Simonella, from
Baton Rouge.

HOMER. Haven't I met you all before?

CALLAHAN. I don't believe so.

HOMER. Something about a dog?

LIZARD. *(laughing up a fuss)* Dog? My word, we don't have
a dog.

HOMER. My memory's as sharp as a tack. It'll come to me
soon enough.

CALLAHAN. I'm sure it will. Hope it doesn't stick you in the
wrong place.

*(**LIZARD** pretends to find this funny)*

Thank you, Darlin', she thinks I have a good sense of
humor. Important when you're plannin' on spending
your life together. You see, Sarah and myself are itch-
ing to get married this afternoon if we can find a dear
old black preacher who married Sarah's mom and dad.

HOMER. What's his name?

CALLAHAN. Now that's the very thing. We forgot to ask.
And both of Sarah's folks are dead now so it's kind of
difficult to ask them. But we do know that he only has
one eye.

HOMER. You folks don't want HIM to marry you.

CALLAHAN. Then you know him? *(to* **LIZARD***)* That's wonderful, isn't it sweetheart?

HOMER. I don't believe you heard me. You don't want him marrying you.

CALLAHAN. Of course we do. Is he all booked up?

HOMER. You might say that, mister. He's booked all right. He's cooling his heels in this very jail.

CALLAHAN. Well, can we at least visit with him? Maybe when he gets out...

HOMER. He ain't gettin' out. And he don't get no visitors. Parish policy when there's a capital offense involved.

CALLAHAN. What are you talkin' about?

HOMER. Reverend Ephraim Smith is charged with willfully murdering, or causing to be murdered, one black female who lived in an orchard on his property east of Newllano.

*(MUSIC IN: **THE SILVER BOWL**)*

He's being arraigned tomorrow mornin' at nine. Open to the public if you want to come. But come early, gonna be a packed house.

*(**CALLAHAN** and **LIZARD** walk away from the courthouse, stripping off their costumes in silence. **LIZARD** drops down and sits.)*

CALLAHAN. You did what you could do, Lizard. More than most people would've done.

LIZARD. But not enough.

(beat)

She's the only one who never asked me about my face.

*(**LIZARD** breaks down crying. **CALLAHAN** takes him into his arms and cradles him.)*

(Lights shift. We are back at the courthouse the next morning.)

*(MUSIC IN: **THE BALLAD OF LIZARD**)*

(People are shuffling past **LIZARD** *and* **CALLAHAN**, *sitting on the steps, waiting to go in.)*

KNUTE. *(to* **CALLAHAN**, *jovial)* Hell of a day to be cooped up in jail, ain't it?

CALLAHAN. Too hot to be anywhere.

KNUTE. Come down here to see the preacher?

(no response)

Biggest case ever hit this town.

(to a woman)

Mornin' Bess. See you made it.

BESS. Oh sure, I knew that preacher was crazy. Whiskey will do that to any man after awhile. But shoot, who'd a thought he'd kill a girl like that.

(beat)

I'm certain they're gonna hang him.

KNUTE. Hasn't been a hangin' since '36. Black man raped a white woman. I hear it sounds like a stick crackin'.

LIZARD. What does?

KNUTE. The sound of the neck breaking.

(laughing)

I'm lookin' forward to that.

(SFX: Morning bells signal nine o'clock.)

BESS. Better get inside. They're gonna be movin' him any minute.

KNUTE. You folks have a good day.

(They disappear into the courthouse.)

CALLAHAN. You ready to go in?

LIZARD. No. I'm gonna stay out here. I don't want to see that man.

CALLAHAN. Alright, but you stay right out here 'til I come out. Then we'll talk about what we're gonna do next.

*(***CALLAHAN*** crosses into the courthouse.)*

(**LIZARD** *climbs the tree and stares into the sky. The light illuminates his body in a shaft from the sun.*)

(*He takes out his skink and pets it as the courthouse empties out onto the street.*)

(**HOMER** *and* **KNUTE**, *on either side of the* **PREACHER**, *walk right past* **LIZARD**. *He and the* **PREACHER** *lock eyes. They lead him off.*)

(**CALLAHAN** *exits the courthouse with his arm around* **RAIN**. **LIZARD** *sees her and practically falls out of the tree.*)

(*MUSIC IN:* **WHATEVER I DID KNOW**)

(**RAIN** *steps in to* **LIZARD**, *who approaches her cautiously.*)

LIZARD. *(to* **RAIN***)* Are you an angel? Can anyone else see you? What's it like where you are?

RAIN. Same as where you are.

(beat)

I'm not DEAD! I'm right here.

(**LIZARD** *reaches out, feels her arm and lifts her into the air with excitement.*)

LIZARD. But I thought he killed you.

RAIN. No. He killed mama. After you left I found her bones in the cave and took 'em to the Sheriff. They came and took the preacher away and I never saw him again. Not 'til today.

(beat)

Are you alright?

LIZARD. Considerin' I thought I saw a ghost I think I'm pretty good.

(beat)

Are you okay?

RAIN. Considerin' everything, I'm fine. I'm goin' to live with Aunt Eunice in Detroit. I leave tomorrow.

(beat)

How was "The Magician and the Slave?"

LIZARD. We only did one performance.

CALLAHAN. One was plenty, as it turned out.

*(**LIZARD** and **RAIN** laugh and run to the upper platform ["the dock"])*

That afternoon I agreed to be responsible for Rain so the three of us could take one last trip to the pump house. Watchin' them look for crawfish was more fun than I'd had in years.

*(**RAIN** grabs **LIZARD** and the two of them run off, laughing all the way. They end in a shaft of light, looking out over the lake.)*

RAIN. I don't know what it's gonna be like in Detroit. I just hope they have good swamp meat, that's all I'm sayin'.

*(**RAIN** begins poking the mud for crawfish. [This is done in pantomime] She sticks her hand deep into the water and pulls one out, throwing it onto the planks.)*

*(**LIZARD** tries to do what she's doing.)*

Be careful Lizard, don't gig 'em. You'll spoil the meat. The gumbo'll be ruined.

LIZARD. Sorry.

RAIN. That's okay. Just take your time. We got all day together. I wanna enjoy every minute of it.

*(**RAIN** reaches in deeper than **LIZARD** and pulls a crawfish out bigger than anything **LIZARD**'s ever seen. She holds it in his face, and the two of them roll on top of one another, wrestling with the crawfish.)*

(After a bit, they stop and look into one another's eyes.)

LIZARD. You think we'll ever see each other after today?

RAIN. If we want to we will.

LIZARD. I want to.

RAIN. Then we will.

LIZARD. Oh, I almost forgot.

(**LIZARD** *pulls out the silver bowl and gives it to her.*)

(*MUSIC IN:* ***THE SILVER BOWL***)

(**RAIN** *takes the bowl and pretends to fill it with water. She goes through the ritual [all without saying a word].*)

CALLAHAN. Right before we headed back into town, they took me to their secret cave and told me all about the Silver Bowl. I looked at Lizard, wondering if he was gonna tell Rain that it was just a story, that the bowl wasn't really silver and that it wasn't worth more than ten dollars.

(**LIZARD** *looks at* **CALLAHAN** *and shakes his head "no".*)

CALLAHAN. *(cont'd)* But somewhere deep down Lizard knew that some dreams needed to stay in place.

LIZARD & RAIN.
WOULDN'T IT BE GOOD IF TIME STOOD STILL
ONE WISH AND YOU'D STAY JUST THIS WAY UNTIL
I WAS READY TO UNDERSTAND THESE THINGS I FEEL

(**CALLAHAN** *enters with their bags. He gives one to* **RAIN**. *She hugs* **LIZARD** *and starts off, stops and runs back, holding onto* **LIZARD** *for a very long time.*)

RAIN. You'll write to me? Tell me about all your adventures.

LIZARD. Sure.

RAIN. And maybe you can come visit us sometime. Or even do a play or somethin' in Detroit.

LIZARD. You never know.

(**RAIN** *gives* **LIZARD** *one last hug and runs off.*)

(**LIZARD** *picks up his backpack and starts to put it on. He turns to* **CALLAHAN** *with a new found maturity.*)

Where to next? Where're we meetin' up with Sally?

CALLAHAN. Actually, Sally's back in DeRitter. She went to talk to Miss Cooley.

LIZARD. Miss Cooley's not in DeRitter anymore. She lives with Mr. Broussard.

CALLAHAN. No. That didn't work out. She's back at the L&N and she wants you to come home.

LIZARD. I don't have a home.

*(**LIZARD** starts to walk away.)*

CALLAHAN. Where you goin'?

LIZARD. I can tell you where I'm not goin'!

CALLAHAN. *(beat)* Look, I can't just let you take off by yourself like this. When you're older it'll be different.

LIZARD. You didn't care how old I was when you took me to Birmingham.

CALLAHAN. Lizard, we're goin' back home ourselves. We can't take you with us. I don't know what's gonna happen with Sally 'n me. I don't even know where I'm gonna wind up.

LIZARD. That's what's so excitin' about life. Findin' out where you're gonna wind up. So long as we stay together...

CALLAHAN. Lizard. I'm sorry. I got no choice.

LIZARD. Everyone has a choice.

CALLAHAN. Sally n' I wanna take you home.

(beat)

To your mother.

*(MUSIC IN: **FULL CIRCLE**)*

LIZARD. She ain't my mother. I don't care if she brought me into this world. She didn't want me. She didn't want anyone to know I was hers. I'm not goin' back there.

CALLAHAN. So where you gonna go then?

(He sings.)

(FULL CIRCLE)

YOU CAN'T KEEP RUNNIN', NO ONE CAN
YOU'LL KEEP FINDIN' THE SAME TOMORROWS

CALLAHAN.

> BUT SOMEWHERE BACK WHERE IT ALL BEGAN
> LIVES YOUR JOY WITH YOUR PAIN AND SORROWS
> ALL WRAPPED UP IN SOMETHIN' THAT YOU WON'T EVEN
>   KNOW
> WITH A LADY WHO HID IT, NEVER DID LET IT SHOW
>
> AND YOU KNOW THAT YOU HAVE TO GO BACK
> OR YOU'LL KEEP SLIPPIN' OFF OF THE TRACK
>
> CAUSE YOU CAN'T BE YOURSELF
> 'TIL YOU KNOW WHO YOU ARE
> AND YOU CAN'T HEAL THE WOUND
> 'TIL YOU DEAL WITH THE SCAR
> AND YOU CAN'T GET AWAY
> NO MATTER HOW FAR YOU ROAM
> CAUSE IT ALL ENDS UP
> WHERE IT ALL BEGAN, HOME

LIZARD. It don't feel like home anymore. Nothin' feels like home anymore.

CALLAHAN. Yeah, that's what happens.

> *(beat)*

> You get farther and farther away from what you know. You make plans, they don't work out. You think you got the answers and then the questions change on you.

> *(beat)*

> But you, Lizard, you're close enough to the past to go back and figure it out.

LIZARD. But what if she don't want me? What if her life is better without me?

CALLAHAN. I can't imagine that possibility.

LIZARD. But what if?

CALLAHAN. Why don't we leave the 'what ifs' 'til tomorrow.

> *(he sings)*

> CAUSE YOU CAN'T LEARN TO WALK
> 'TIL YOU LEARN HOW TO CRAWL
> AND YOU CAN'T LEARN TO RUN

'TIL YOU LEARN TO WALK TALL
AND YOU WON'T EVER FLY
'TIL YOU'VE DEALT WITH IT ALL
AND YOU'VE TAKEN THE FALLS IN BETWEEN

AND YOU CAN'T LEARN TO DANCE
IF YOU DON'T FEEL THE SONG
AND YOU WON'T KNOW WHAT'S RIGHT
'TIL YOU KNOW WHAT WENT WRONG

AND YOU CAN'T FIND YOUR PLACE
'TIL YOU'RE WHERE YOU BELONG
YOU CAN TRAVEL TO CHINA OR ROME
BUT YOU'LL ALWAYS END UP
WHERE IT ALL BEGAN, HOME

(The song brings us back to the L&N Cafe in DeRidder.)

(MISS COOLEY *enters and steps into* **LIZARD***. She is very emotional and struggles with her impulse to take him in her arms.)*

(As she steps forward, **LIZARD** *steps away from her and scurries up the tree.* **MISS COOLEY** *turns back to* **CALLAHAN***.)*

MISS COOLEY. *(indicating Sally)* I already explained all this to her. You had no right to take him away from that place.

CALLAHAN. He didn't belong there.

MISS COOLEY. And you don't belong here. I could have you arrested for kidnapping the boy.

(looking up at **LUCIUS***)*

So he knows I'm his mother? What else does he know?

CALLAHAN. He knows that his father's alive.

MISS COOLEY. Then he knows more than I do.

CALLAHAN. On his birth certificate it said...

MISS COOLEY. I was barely seventeen when I filled out that paper. I wrote what I wanted to write.

CALLAHAN. How come you didn't tell Lucius you were his mother?

MISS COOLEY. Okay, listen, if he was retarded bad as everybody said, the less he knew the better, right? And if he wasn't retarded, he'd figure it out soon enough.

CALLAHAN. But why'd you give him up? I can't understand...

MISS COOLEY. Nobody wants to get tied down to somebody has a boy like Lucius. I tried to put it all behind me. I wasn't gonna tell Alton. I swear I wasn't. But I couldn't keep the secret. Soon as he knew about Lucius, he put his foot down. I thought he would soften over time. I could convince him. I begged him to let Lucius come with us. I did! He wouldn't have any of it.

CALLAHAN. So you sent him away.

MISS COOLEY. But I went back to get him. I went back. And he was gone. I knew it wasn't right and then he was gone, and I thought so many things might'a happened to him...

(She breaks down.)

Sometimes it just gets where you don't know what to do, where to turn. You think you're doin' the right thing and then...

*(She looks up at **LIZARD**)*

He talk to you?

CALLAHAN. He talks a lot.

MISS COOLEY. Really? He never talks to me.

(yelling up to the tree)

Lucius!

(beat)

Why don't you come inside and get something to eat.

(silence)

Lucius, I'm talking to you, son.

LIZARD. My name is Lizard now.

MISS COOLEY. Is it? Well things do change, don't they. Still, you ought to come in.

LIZARD. It's too early to come in.

MISS COOLEY. Suit yourself. Just don't let the mosquitoes eat you up out here.

(to SALLY)

I'm gonna go pack you something to eat for your trip.

(she begins to exit, turns to LIZARD)

I'm glad you came back. I missed you.

(MISS COOLEY exits. SALLY motions to CALLAHAN to talk to LIZARD. She follows SALLY off.)

CALLAHAN. So you gonna come down out of there to say goodbye or what?

LIZARD. *(climbing down)* I'm comin' with you. I decided. I don't care what you say.

CALLAHAN. That's not gonna work, Lizard.

LIZARD. Why not? We can all work together and open a theatre maybe. You said I was good.

CALLAHAN. Yeah, too good. I'm not gonna let you be on stage with me again.

LIZARD. I want to come with you.

(LIZARD rushes to CALLAHAN and hugs him. There is a long moment.)

CALLAHAN. You know somethin' Lizard. If I was ever gonna have me a son, I'd want him to be just like you.

LIZARD. Then why don't you want me to come with you?

CALLAHAN. It's not that I don't want you to come with me. It's just, I think your mamma needs you more than I do.

LIZARD. She doesn't need me. She never needed me.

(SALLY enters with her bag.)

SALLY. We better get goin' if we want to get some miles in before it gets dark.

(MISS COOLEY enters with some wrapped plates of food. LIZARD moves away.)

MISS COOLEY. Here you are. Thanks for bringin' him back.

 (to **LIZARD***)*

You want me to put your skink in his cage.

LIZARD. No. Thank you.

 *(***LIZARD*** looks to* **CALLAHAN***, and then turns away, realizing that he has to stay put.)*

MISS COOLEY. Lucius, Lizard...I'm sorry for what I done. You don't have to do it right away but I hope you'll forgive me.

 *(***MISS COOLEY*** breaks down, stuck in place.* **LIZARD** *crosses to her and the two hug.)*

CALLAHAN. You take care of that lizard. I wanna see him all growed up when I come back.

 *(***SALLY*** crosses to* **LIZARD** *and hugs him.* **CALLAHAN** *and* **SALLY** *exit.* **LIZARD** *climbs the tree as* **MISS COOLEY** *looks on.)*

MISS COOLEY. Don't stay out here too long. I want to hear all about your travels.

 (She exits.)

 *(***LIZARD*** looks around from atop the tree.)*

 *(***CALLAHAN*** appears in a pool of light. They sing.)*

CALLAHAN & LIZARD.

 CAUSE YOU CAN'T LEARN TO WALK
 'TIL YOU LEARN HOW TO CRAWL
 AND YOU CAN'T LEARN TO RUN
 'TIL YOU LEARN TO WALK TALL

 AND YOU WON'T EVER FLY
 'TIL YOU'VE DEALT WITH IT ALL
 AND YOU'VE TAKEN THE FALLS IN BETWEEN

 (The company enters and continues singing.)

 *(***LIZARD*** climbs down and crosses to* **MISS COOLEY***, sitting at a table. He sits across from her and starts talking...telling her his stories.)*

COMPANY.

AND YOU CAN'T BE YOURSELF
'TIL YOU KNOW WHO YOU ARE
AND YOU CAN'T HEAL THE WOUND
'TIL YOU DEAL WITH THE SCAR
AND YOU CAN'T GET AWAY
NO MATTER HOW FAR YOU ROAM
CAUSE IT ALWAYS ENDS UP
WHERE IT ALL BEGAN, HOME.

THE END

OTHER TITLES AVAILABLE FROM SAMUEL FRENCH

YO HO HO: A PIRATE'S CHRISTMAS

Book by James J. Mellon
Music and Lyrics by James J. Mellon
and Scott DeTurk

Holiday Musical / 2m, 2f, plus 7m/f, 3f children, 1 m/f child

It's up to a little seven year-old girl named Eve to save Christmas for everyone! What will become of Christmas when Santa Claus and the citizens of the North Pole are kidnapped by a bunch of directionally challenged pirates? This wondrous musical is destined to become a holiday tradition for you and your entire family.

"*Yo Ho Ho! A Pirate's Christmas* is old-fashioned jolly fun tweaked with a sense of adventure!"
— *Canyon News*

"CRITIC'S PICK! A hidden treasure with something appealing for every age group. A little ho-ho-ho turns into a lot of fun-fun-fun at Yo-Ho-Ho! This is one family show that you won't want to miss!"
— *Pam Vetter, Los Angeles Chronicle*

OTHER TITLES AVAILABLE FROM SAMUEL FRENCH

THE PEOPLE VS. MONA

Jim Wann and Patricia Miller

Musical / 3m, 5f (w/ doubling; expandable casting options) / Unit Set

The People vs. Mona is a love story, murder mystery, courtroom shenanigans, fate-of-a-small-town-hanging-on-the-verdict musical.

For professional companies: seven actor/singers play all the roles in a multicultural cast, accompanied by three onstage musicians. For high schools, colleges, and community theatre: the cast may be expanded by having one actor in each witness role, and a chorus of townspeople in the larger numbers.

The music combines folk, blues, gospel, jazz, rock, musical comedy, school anthem, marching band and bossa nova with a theatrical sensibility.

Mona Mae Katt, a third-generation Latina-American, owns the Frog Pad, the long-time musical heart of Tippo, GA, a town in need of a plan to revive itself. She is accused of killing C.C. Katt, recording studio operator and her husband of ten hours, by hitting him over the head with her Stratocaster guitar. She is defended by Jim Summerford, a Southern gentleman who's never won a case against prosecutor and Mayoral candidate Mavis Frye—his fiancé.

As Jim tries to prove Mona's innocence, he becomes attracted to her, and Mavis ups the stakes: she wants to convict Mona, marry Jim, take office, tear down the Frog Pad, and put up a Casino—bringing in bucks, but taking away Tippo's artistic and social traditions in the process. And if Mona is found guilty, the odds are Mavis will get her way.

Several of the actors play multiple roles in a parade of witnesses on the way to a sequence of surprise endings. MONA manages to combine a love triangle, courtroom drama, and character-driven comedy in an original book musical, with a light-hearted message about the importance of cultural heritage in America's towns. Keep the Frog Pad alive!

OTHER TITLES AVAILABLE FROM SAMUEL FRENCH

SHINE!: THE HORATIO ALGER MUSICAL

Book by Richard Seff
Music by Roger Anderson
Lyrics by Lee Goldsmith

13m, 6f / Various sets

**Winner! 2010 New York Musical Theatre Festival Award
for Excellence
Winner! National Music Theatre Network Award!**

This charming rags to riches romp with a melodic score follows Ragged Dick, Horatio Alger's first best selling hero, from penniless bootblack to budding Wall Street entrepreneur. His adventures bring him face to face with scheming ex convicts, vicious comic villians, kind benefactors and a world of colorful street characters. Set in the New York Centennial summer of 1876, this full of hopes and dreams musical is perfect for the whole family.

"A charming, feel-good musical. The work's tremendous heart and unabashed celebration of Alger's popular stories are in ample evidence in this appealing musical about the rise from rags to riches."
– Meredith Lee, *TheaterMania*

"Awfully close to the sort of musical that made the form nationally beloved in the Rodgers and Hammerstein era."
– Marc Miller, *Backstage*

"Highly tuneful...A friendly show of considerable good humor."
– *Playbill*

OTHER TITLES AVAILABLE FROM SAMUEL FRENCH

ABE

Book and Lyrics by Lee Goldsmith
Music by Roger Anderson

Musical / 16m, 9f

Abe is a new musical about the early life of Abraham Lincoln. The show explores his youth as a flatboat pilot on the Mississippi, his early love for Ann Rutledge, his troubled marriage to the difficult and mentally fragile Mary Todd, and his attempt to be a good father to his sons. The story follows Abe from his earliest attempts at self-improvement through the 1860 election which made him the 16th president of an already fracturing United States.

The score is fully orchestrated and uses bold, melodic and traditional musical theatre styles that embrace the story's period and Americana roots. It can be produced fully staged or as a concert performance. The musical features a large cast and requires strong singers: baritone, soprano, mezzo-soprano, 3 adult male singing roles, 3 male children singing roles, male/female chorus with many speaking roles.

"The founding fathers got their own musical with *1776*, so
why not *Abe?*"
- Playbill.com